Wyoming
Special Delivery

Melissa Senate

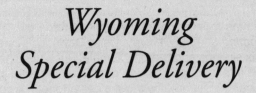

HARLEQUIN
SPECIAL
EDITION

Special thanks and acknowledgment are given to Melissa Senate for her contribution to the Dawson Family Ranch miniseries.

HARLEQUIN®
SPECIAL EDITION™

Recycling programs for this product may not exist in your area.

ISBN-13: 978-1-335-89448-9

Wyoming Special Delivery

He stood up. "I'd shake your hand if both weren't occupied. You have a deal, Ms. Dawson."

Relief settled on her face. "Thank you. Neither of us will regret this."

"We'll see," he said. "I should warn you, Daisy. I do mean to take ownership of the ranch. Liking you people and this place or not. I want to be very clear on that."

She lifted her chin. "Five days," she said.

"Five days," he repeated.

She nodded, did some kind of wizardry with the sling and settled Tony back inside, then extended her hand.

He shook it, the feel of her soft, warm hand in his unexpectedly...charged.

"Let's begin with a tour of the ranch," she said. "You've barely seen the place."

"Okay," he agreed. "A tour of the ranch."

It's one little walk. She'll show you the lodge and the cafeteria. She'll talk about her grandparents. You'll nod. You'll go your separate ways in a half hour.

Repeat for five days.

He could get through this. Intact. He was 75 percent sure.

* * *

DAWSON FAMILY RANCH:
Life, love, legacy in Wyoming.

Dear Reader,

The nine-months-pregnant single heroine of *Wyoming Special Delivery*, Daisy Dawson, is one of six siblings and the only female. But when she goes into labor on the side of a Wyoming road in the dead of summer without a cell phone or a spare brother, she's beyond grateful when the handsome, mysterious guest at her family's dude ranch turns up—and delivers her baby boy.

But Harrison McCord has a secret reason for staying at the Dawson Family Ranch. A reason Daisy will not like one bit. Bringing her newborn son into the world, though, changes *everything* for the both of them.

I hope you enjoy Daisy and Harrison's story. Feel free to write me with any comments or questions at MelissaSenate@yahoo.com and visit my website, melissasenate.com for more info about me and my books. For lots of photos of my cat and dog, friend me over on Facebook.

Happy spring and happy reading!

Warmest regards,

Melissa Senate

Melissa Senate has written many novels for Harlequin and other publishers, including her debut, *See Jane Date*, which was made into a TV movie. She also wrote seven books for Harlequin's Special Edition line under the pen name Meg Maxwell. Her novels have been published in over twenty-five countries. Melissa lives on the coast of Maine with her teenage son; their rescue shepherd mix, Flash; and a lap cat named Cleo. For more information, please visit her website, melissasenate.com.

Books by Melissa Senate

Harlequin Special Edition

Dawson Family Ranch
For the Twins' Sake

The Wyoming Multiples
The Baby Switch!
Detective Barelli's Legendary Triplets
Wyoming Christmas Surprise
To Keep Her Baby
A Promise for the Twins

Furever Yours
A New Leash on Love

Montana Mavericks: Six Brides for Six Brothers
Rust Creek Falls Cinderella

Montana Mavericks: The Great Family Roundup (as Meg Maxwell)
Mommy and the Maverick

Montana Mavericks: The Lonelyhearts Ranch
The Maverick's Baby-in-Waiting

Visit the Author Profile page
at Harlequin.com for more titles.

Chapter One

Daisy Dawson's wedding ceremony was supposed to start any minute, and there was no sign of the groom. At nine months pregnant, in a pretty but scratchy white lace maternity dress and peau de soie heels that pinched, standing around wasn't exactly easy.

She poked her head out the door of the small room where she was getting ready. The special events hall of the Dawson Family Guest Ranch lodge had been beautifully decorated, thanks to her sister-in-law, Sara, who'd gone all out with pink and red roses, white tulle, and a red satin carpet runner to create an aisle. Thirty-six chairs were set up on both sides of the carpet. On the bride's side, she saw her five brothers in the first row, all decked out in suits and Stetsons and cowboy boots. She saw her colleagues from the ranch. She saw old friends and newer ones.

But the other side of the aisle was still conspicuously empty of guests. No relatives or friends of the groom had arrived. That was really weird. Jacob was late and so were all the people he'd invited to their wedding?

Sure, Daisy. Right.

She poked her head back in and looked in the mirror, reality hitting her right in the nose. Jacob wasn't coming to his own wedding. And since none of his guests had turned up, it was obvious that he'd let them know in advance that he was calling it off. How kind of him to tell everyone in his life but her.

Everyone who meant something special to her was waiting for her to walk down the aisle. And there wasn't going to be a wedding. She shook her head, calling herself all kinds of a fool for ever thinking this was going to happen.

Ping!

Daisy eyed her phone on the vanity table with all her cosmetics and the curling iron she'd painstakingly used to get beachy waves in her straight light brown hair. The text was either from one of her brothers asking if everything was okay—since the ceremony was supposed to start at 5:00 p.m.—or it was her fiancé, Jacob, the cowardly fink, not facing her in person.

She grabbed her phone. It was Jacob.

I'm really sorry. But it hit me hard this morning that we don't love each other and we've been forcing it. And I've been forcing that I can be a dad. I'm heading back to Cheyenne and might move east. Wish you and the baby all the best. J.

A burst of sadness got her in the heart at the same time that red-hot anger seized her. She stared at herself in the mirror, through her late mother's beautiful lace veil, which she should have known would be bad luck. She'd tried, at least. Tried, tried, tried all summer to make it work with Jacob—she'd thought they were going to build a future together. A family. But her baby wouldn't have a father.

She stuffed her phone in her little beaded cross-body purse and stalked out the back door and down the side steps, to where her Honda, with a Just Married sign with streamers on the back, waited to get her out of here.

She quickly got in the car and took a deep breath, flipped back the veil, then texted her brother Noah.

J called off the wedding. Need some time alone.

She reread Jacob's text. Wish you and the baby all the best. Like he was some distant uncle! How dare he? She banged the phone against the steering wheel and chucked it out the window, then pulled off her engagement ring and threw it out, too. She grabbed the headpiece and veil off her head and tossed them on the back seat.

Then she peeled out, seeing the ridiculous streamers floating behind the car in the rearview mirror as she took off down the drive toward the gates of the ranch.

Where exactly am I going? she wondered, trying not to cry so she wouldn't swerve into the wildflowers lining the road. She lived in the main house at the guest ranch, and no way could she deal with relative after relative, friend after friend coming to see her, feeling sorry for her. So forget about her sanctuary of her bedroom and pulling the quilt over her head for a few days.

Jacob had booked a weekend honeymoon for the two of them at the Starlight B&B in Prairie City, a half hour away. She supposed she could go there and lick her wounds and order their highly rated room service. Her cravings were insane these days. All she seemed to want was pasta in pink sauce with bacon and peas. And garlic bread. And chocolate cake. All B&Bs had chocolate cake, right?

Thinking of the food almost took her mind off being stood up at the altar and the sudden change to her future.

Not just hers. Her brothers' futures, too. Four of the five Dawson men had scattered across Wyoming, and she'd been hoping to steer them back home to stay. She'd had big plans for becoming a secret amateur matchmaker at the wedding reception tonight, putting individually irresistible women for the four remaining Dawson bachelors under their unsuspecting noses. But some case she could make to Ford, Axel, Zeke and Rex for sticking around Bear Ridge, finding true love and settling down in their hometown, if not on their home ranch, *now*.

One of her brothers—Noah—had already done exactly that, which had given Daisy hope for the others. One down, five to go, right? Her wedding had brought them all home when being at the ranch, being in Bear Ridge, made them all feel… unsettled. But they'd inherited the ranch last winter from their father, and only Noah had stayed to rebuild the long-closed, run-down family business.

Daisy, then five months pregnant and alone, had joined Noah in the mission, and no one had been more surprised than her when her baby's father had come after her, saying he was sorry, that he wanted a second chance, that they could do this, after all: be a family. He'd lasted four months.

She'd thought she was getting married today. She'd thought she could convince her brothers that true love really did exist, even if it hadn't for their father and various mothers—there were three moms among the Dawson siblings. She'd thought the Dawson clan could start fresh here together. She'd thought she could use the wedding festivities to show them they could be happy here. Among the guests she'd invited were at least eight women who would seriously appeal to each single brother for one reason or another. Falling in love would be just the ticket back. But after seeing their sister stood up at the altar—nine months pregnant with their little niece or nephew—the four remaining Dawson bachelors would hightail it out of Bear Ridge, which had always meant bad luck to all of them. Family was everything to Daisy. And not only had her dreams of building her own family with her baby's father gone *poof*, but Ford, Axel, Zeke and Rex would most likely leave tonight or tomorrow and come back for her baby's birth, then leave again after a day or two and return for Christmas. Maybe.

Family: the way it wasn't supposed to be.

Daisy let out a sigh and kept driving, teary acceptance and pissed-as-hell fighting for dominance. Fifteen minutes later, the two still going at it, she drove down the service road on the outskirts of Bear Ridge that would eventually lead her to the freeway. But then her car made a weird sputtering sound. *Crunch-creak.* Then another. *Crunch-creeeeeeeak.*

Oh no. She quickly pulled over, turned off the engine, then tried to restart. Nothing.

"Nooo!" she yelped, hitting the steering wheel. *Someone tell me this is all a bad dream.* She looked around, out the windshield and both passenger windows. She was on some rural stretch, hay bales for acres on either side of her. Not another car in sight. She tried the ignition again. Dead. One more time, because you never knew. Still dead.

She rested her head against the steering wheel for a moment, the stretch tearing the side of her wedding gown. Fine with her. The minute she got to the Starlight, she'd be rolling it up in a wad and setting it on fire in a garbage can out front like she was Angela Bassett in *Waiting to Exhale*.

This really wasn't her day after all.

Daisy grabbed her purse to get her phone to call for help, then grimaced. "Oh hell, that was stupid." Her phone was behind the rosebushes on the side of the lodge. With her engagement ring. Her mom had often said, *Daisy Rae Dawson, acting first and thinking later is gonna be your downfall, sweetcakes.* Her beloved mother was right about that. Especially now.

She sat there for a second, taking another breath when she was hit with a strange, pulling sensation low in her belly. That was weird. She grabbed her stomach and started breathing the way she'd learned in Lamaze class. A minute or so later, it hit her again. *Oh no. No, no, no.* Were these contractions? Maybe they were the false early ones the Lamaze teacher had mentioned yesterday, when Jacob was there breathing deeply beside her, making her believe he was really committed to her and their child. She wasn't due for another three weeks!

The pain got more intense. She stared at her silver watch with the mother-of-pearl face, a gift from her brothers for Christmas last year. The sweeping second hand told her the contractions were coming every minute and a half.

She was in labor. Left-at-the-altar, three-weeks-early labor.

Without a phone. On the side of the road. In rural Wyoming.

She got out of the car as another contraction sent her gripping the side of the door for support. She stared up and down the road, praying a vehicle would come by. Without an ax murderer in it.

She started pacing, keeping one hand on the car, but it was July and eighty-two degrees and the car was hot. Contraction! She bent over and let out the scream bursting from her. "Owww-weeee!"

Breathe, breathe, breathe, she reminded herself. She heard the sound of rushing wheels in the distance. A car! Yes! It was coming closer! She managed to pick up her head to look. Oh, thank God. Someone was coming and stopping behind her car.

A fancy silver SUV with Wyoming plates. Not one of her brothers' cars. Or anyone she knew. One of the guests at the ranch had a fancy silver SUV, now that she thought about it.

"Owww-weeee!" She yelped and doubled over as the contraction seized her.

She heard a car door open and close, footsteps rushing toward her.

"I'll help you get in my SUV," a male voice said, coming closer. "I'm not a stranger," he added quickly as he bent down where she stood to sort of make eye contact. "I'm a guest at Dawson's ranch."

She glanced up. It *was* him. He might not be a stranger or an ax murderer, but he *was* kind of mysterious. He'd been at the ranch for two days yet didn't seem remotely interested in the horses or activities. She'd even mentioned to Noah, the foreman, that something was up with the guest who'd booked Cabin No. 1, which slept four, all for himself, and then hadn't gotten on a horse the entire time he was here.

Maybe he *was* an ax murderer.

"No time," she managed to croak out as she dropped to her knees, then backward onto her butt. "The baby…is…*coming*! Owww-weeee!"

Over her earsplitting yelp, she still heard him gasp and saw him grab his phone, then listened to him frantically explain the situation to the 911 dispatcher.

"Okay," he was saying into the phone with accompanying nodding. "Okay. Okay. Okay, I think I can do that. Okay."

"Owww-weeee!" she screamed, eyes squeezed shut as she bore down.

"Oh God," he said, rushing to kneel in front of her.

He lifted up her wedding dress and cast it over her knees. She heard him run away and thought *noo, don't leave me*, but then he was back, and she realized he was cutting off her ridiculous lace maternity undies with a Swiss army knife.

She had the urge to bear down again. And grunted and did.

"The ambulance is coming," he assured her. "Just hang on, Daisy."

"I'll try," she said, squeezing her eyes shut. "But I can't!" she croaked out, opening her eyes. "You're…about…to…*owww-weeee*…deliver my… baby!" she yelped.

Harrison McCord's brain fought to catch up with what was happening. Not forty-five minutes ago, he'd seen Daisy, all decked out in bridal wear, walk into the ranch lodge with another woman who he recognized as her sister-in-law. Now, Daisy was still in the wedding dress, which was dirty in some spots along the bottom. But she was alone, no rings on her finger, he noticed, on the side of a road. And, if he wasn't mistaken, *in labor.* What the heck had happened between then and this minute?

"What can I do?" he asked, his voice frantic.

"Get…these pinching shoes…off me!" she barked out before leaning back and shouting, "Owww-weeee!" That was followed by four fast breaths. Then four more.

He took the white shoes off her feet, and her face relaxed for a second, then the panting, grunting and yelping, and breathing started again.

"The baby. Is. Coming!" she screamed. She scrunched up her face.

"Oh God," he said. Again he lifted the long lacy gown and flung the edge up over her knees. He could see the baby's head. Whoa.

He forgot everything the dispatcher had said. *What the hell do I do?* Instinct must have taken over, because he took off his dress shirt and held it carefully under the head as he guided the baby—a boy—out. He then gently wrapped the messy newborn in his shirt and handed him to Daisy.

"It's a boy!" he announced.

Her mouth opened in a kind of wonder as she took the newborn and held him against her, tears running down her cheeks.

He heard sirens in the distance, coming closer. "That's the ambulance," he said, relief flooding him. It pulled up in front of Daisy's car, and two guys and a woman jumped out, one wheeling a stretcher. An EMT took the baby while the other two helped Daisy onto the stretcher.

"Thank you so much," she said to Harrison, her blue eyes misty. "Thank you."

"Of course." His heart was beating a zillion

miles a minute. He had to sit down before he passed out.

"Call my brother Noah, the foreman at the ranch," she shouted out to him as the EMTs loaded her into the back of the ambulance.

"Will do!" he called back.

He'd just delivered a baby. On the side of the road. He was grateful he'd been wearing a T-shirt under his dress shirt or he'd have helped bring the newborn into the world half-naked.

The ambulance making a racket as it drove away, he was stirred to action. He pulled out his phone and called the guest ranch and asked for foreman Noah Dawson's cell phone number, adding that it was an emergency. He'd been watching Noah the past couple of days. Daisy, too. Watching everything. Unfortunately, the Dawsons seemed like good people. But as his dad used to say, that was neither here nor there.

He punched in Noah's number. He answered right away.

"Noah Dawson. What's the emergency?"

"This is Harrison McCord from Cabin No. 1," he said. "I just helped deliver your sister Daisy's baby on the side of the service road onto Route 26. She doesn't seem to have a phone with her. The ambulance took her to Prairie City General."

"What?" Noah bellowed. "Is the baby okay? Is Daisy okay?"

"They both seemed fine," he said. "It's a boy, by the way."

"We're on our way. Thanks for helping Daisy."

Harrison pocketed his phone and got back in his car, just sitting there behind the wheel for a moment, barely able to process what had just happened. A single workaholic businessman, he had no siblings to provide baby nieces and nephews, and he didn't think he'd ever held a baby in his life—until today.

He drove the fifteen minutes to Prairie City and pulled into a spot in the hospital parking lot, then stopped in the gift shop. There were congratulations balloons, get-well balloons and an entire section devoted to stuffed animals, big and small. He eyed a soft and squishy medium-sized light brown teddy bear with a plaid bow tie and bought it, then followed the signs to Maternity.

In the elevator he stared at the bear, unable to fully comprehend how he'd ended up here, holding this stuffed toy, about to visit a new mother he hadn't more than nodded at while seeing her at the ranch the past couple of days. A new mother who would hate his guts when she found out why he was really at the ranch.

Daisy was in room 508. He sucked in a breath and peered in the open door. Now in a hospital gown with a thin white blanket covering half of her, she was alone—well, except for the baby in her arms, her gaze so full of wonder as she stared at the infant that he felt he was intruding. He was about to turn around and flee when she said, "You! My hero!"

Harrison offered what had to be an awkward smile and walked fully into the room.

She smiled at him. "I'm sorry—as guest relations manager of the ranch, I'd normally know your name, where you're from, if you like decaf or regular for your cabin, but I took this past week off for the wedding. I wasn't even thinking I'd need to start my maternity leave so soon." She smiled a dazzling smile. Wow, she was pretty. All glowy and happy. "But I do recognize you as one of our guests. Guess you didn't expect your day to go quite like this."

He had to laugh. "Nope. Definitely not. But I'm glad I happened to be driving down that road. You didn't have a phone to call for help?"

She frowned and glanced down at the baby. "As you probably figured out from my outfit and the dumb sign on the back of my car, I was supposed to get married today. The groom, my newborn son's father, didn't show and sent me a Dear Jane text. I got pissed and chucked my phone out the window of my car. Dumb, I know."

The father of her baby had left her at the altar? When she was nine months pregnant?

"Sorry about the wedding," he said, unable to even imagine what that must have felt like. He'd never come close to marrying. Or proposing to anyone. But he'd been betrayed before and knew what *that* felt like.

"I'm sure I dodged a bullet. We weren't right for each other, and we both knew it."

So did he, despite not even having met her before today. Because he'd been keeping watch over the Dawson family and the only two of the six siblings who worked at the ranch, he'd made a point of taking a tailing walk whenever he noticed Daisy strolling a path with the fiancé, a surfer-cowboy type. Their body language was always so awkward. They never held hands or kissed, though they did take a lot of walks on the paths, which was how he managed to spy on them so often. He'd wondered about their relationship because they barely seemed like a couple, yet he'd overheard her tell the fiancé it was time to get to Lamaze yesterday, and off they'd gone.

She waved a hand in front of her. "Anyway.

That is old news. This," she said, smiling down at the baby, "is breaking news and all that matters."

The love and reverence and sincerity in her voice caught him by surprise, and for a moment, he just gazed at the baby with her. Finally, he cleared his throat. "My name is Harrison McCord," he said, stiffly sitting down in the chair by her bed. "I got you a little something. Well, I got him a little something," he added, gesturing at the tiny human lying alongside her arm. The newborn was skinny and cute with wispy brown curls. His eyes were closed at the moment. "I'm in Cabin No. 1 at the ranch. I booked it for the week."

"But it's just you?" she asked. "Cabin No. 1 sleeps four."

"Just me," he said.

She waited a beat, as if she expected him to elaborate, but now was certainly not the time or the place. He'd wait a couple days, give her a chance to settle back at the main house at the ranch with the baby, and then he'd ask for a meeting with her and her brother. And drop a bombshell. The timing wasn't good, but that couldn't he helped.

"So what's his name?" he asked.

"Tony. After my late grandpa, Anthony Dawson. I haven't decided on a middle name," she said.

"Given what you did for me—for *us*—I'd like to use your middle initial."

He gaped at her. *No, no, no, no, no. Noooo.* "That's very thoughtful, but there's no need for that."

"You came to our rescue, Harrison. You helped bring this little guy into the world. I'd like to honor that."

He swallowed, his T-shirt suddenly tight around his neck. "Um, I...don't have a middle name," he lied. He actually did—Leo. "I'd better get going," he added, bolting up. "I did call your brother. He's on the way." He put the teddy bear on the table beside her bed.

She tilted her head at him. "Oh. Okay. Well, thanks again. For everything."

As she turned her attention back to the baby, he took one last look at her, not wanting to leave— but how could he stay? Now that he'd met Daisy Dawson under these unusual circumstances—like delivering her baby and calling her brother and visiting her in the hospital and bringing baby Tony a teddy bear *and* hearing how she'd been left at the altar—he felt something of a connection to the new mother. The news he planned to deliver in a couple days wouldn't be as cut-and-dried as he'd expected.

It's just straight-up, on-paper business, he reminded himself. *Nothing personal.*

She wanted to give her baby his middle initial!

Things with Daisy Dawson had suddenly gotten *very* personal.

Chapter Two

Okay, Cabin No. 1 guest who very unexpectedly helped deliver her baby? Definitely mysterious. Her wanting to use his middle initial for Tony's middle name had him jumping up like an electrocuted porcupine. What was with the guy?

Then again, he'd had a pretty eventful last hour.

"Well, Tony," she said, looking at her baby son. "It's just me and you. And I think I'll use my mother's first initial for your middle name. Her name was Leah. Let's see… Liam. Lucas. Lawrence. Lee, Landon, Lincoln. Louis. Levi. Leonardo DiCaprio." She stared at Tony, thinking he didn't look anything like the actor. "How about

Lester, as in Lester Holt?" she suggested. "Tony Lester Dawson. Tony Lucas Dawson. Tony Lincoln Dawson. Hey," she whispered. "I think we have a winner. Very presidential, right? Anthony Lincoln Dawson, it is."

Luckily she'd gotten the name squared away, because the room suddenly filled with the five Dawson brothers and Sara, her sister-in-law and best friend. There were gasps and oohs and ahhs and so many flowers, balloons and stuffed animals, a few huge, that another person could not squeeze in.

"I present your nephew, Anthony 'Tony' Lincoln Dawson," she said. "Tony for his very special great-grandpa Anthony Dawson." Gramps had always been called Anth, interestingly enough, a nickname started by his mother when he was very young, but the moment Harrison McCord had helped place the newborn on her chest on the side of that road, she'd instantly thought: Tony.

"Gramps would like that," Axel said, and they all nodded reverently.

"The *L* in Lincoln for Mom?" Noah asked with a gentle smile.

Daisy gave a teary nod just thinking what a wonderful nana Leah Dawson would have been. The six Dawson siblings had three mothers among them. Ford from the first marriage, Rex, Zeke and Axel from the second, and Daisy and Noah from the third. The siblings had all gotten to know Daisy and Noah's mother pretty well since she'd been so kind and welcoming that their mothers had felt comfortable dropping them off for weekends and weeks in summer with their not-exactly-attentive father. That had stopped when Leah had died when Daisy was eleven, though. A few hours here and there were all the other two mothers had trusted Bo Dawson with their kids.

"That's really nice, Daisy," Noah said, and she could see how touched he was.

"So Tony for Gramps, Lincoln for my mom, and Dawson because Jacob called off the wedding *and* being a father." She explained about the text. Tossing her phone and engagement ring. And then about her car sputtering on the service road and Harrison McCord coming to her aid.

"We all owe him one," Noah said. "No phone, hot as hell out, rural stretch of road. Thank God he came along."

Daisy nodded. "I kind of wonder why he *did*, though. There's something up with the guy."

"What do you mean?" Ford asked in cop tone. A police officer in Casper, Ford didn't let anything escape his attention.

"Well, Noah can probably attest to how odd it is that a guest would book a cabin for four and then show up solo *and* not partake in a single activity at a dude ranch," Daisy explained. "I've only seen him walking the grounds. In fact, any time I've been out, I feel like he's been around. And then he's suddenly five minutes behind me on the service road to the freeway?"

Noah narrowed his eyes. "You know, now that you mention it, he does seem unusual. He wasn't interested in being matched with a horse. And twice I've looked up while in the barn or talking to the ranch hands, and there'd he'd be, suddenly pulling out his phone like he had to make a call that second."

"Sounds like he's watching you two," Axel said. A search-and-rescue expert, Axel wasn't one to believe in coincidence.

Daisy shrugged. "He did help me, though. And then came to visit me and Tony. He brought this," she added, pointing at the teddy bear. "I told him I wanted to give Tony his middle initial, and he turned white. Said he didn't have a middle name and made excuses to leave."

Rex, the businessman of the brothers, crossed his arms over his chest. "Hmm. Something is definitely up with him. But like you said, he did come to your rescue. You and Tony are safe and healthy."

Noah nodded. "That's all that matters right now."

"Couldn't hurt to check him out," Zeke said. This from the mysterious brother. Zeke had long refused to talk about his work and would only say it was highly classified, whatever that meant. Sometimes Daisy thought he was a spy.

"Couldn't agree more," Ford said, taking out his phone. "What's the guest's name? I'll start with a simple check on the guy. Just to be safe."

"Harrison McCord," Daisy told him. "Wyoming plates. Silver Lexus."

"Harrison McCord," Rex repeated, clearly thinking. "That name does sound familiar. I've heard it before. In business circles, I think." Rex lived out in Jackson, Wyoming, which was hours away from Bear Ridge.

Ford nodded and stepped out of the room, phone in hand. It was good having a cop in the family.

"I'll keep an eye on McCord," Axel said. "Turns out I'll be staying for a week or two. I'm on enforced R&R from my search-and-rescue team."

All eyes turned to Axel. He rarely said so much about his private life. She wondered what had happened to get him sent on "vacation."

"I'd like to stay at the main house with you, Daize," Axel added, "if you'd like the company."

She beamed. She'd be able to work on keeping Axel in town *forever*! She almost wanted to add a mock-evil *mwahaha*, she was so happy about the news. "I'd love it. But you'll be woken up all hours of the night by a shrieking newborn. Just pointing it out if it didn't occur to you."

Axel stared at the creature in her arms, his blue eyes widening slightly as he ran a hand through his thick dark brown hair. "Not like I'll be getting any sleep anyway, so bring it on, little nephew."

Daisy laughed, but as she glanced at Axel, she could see something was eating at him—something about the enforced vacation and whatever had gone down there. He could probably use a little distraction, right? She *would* put her matchmaking plan into action. Within two weeks, he'd never want to leave anyway, because he'd be too in love. With the woman she had in mind for him and with his darling baby nephew, who'd be the apple of his ole eye. He'd sign on with a new search-and-rescue team much closer to Bear Ridge and build a big, gorgeous modern log cabin on the edge of the ranch property. That was the dream—having all her brothers back home.

Yes, Daisy was feeling better about knowing

three of her brothers would be leaving later today or in the morning. Because Noah was here, of course. And now Axel would be, too.

"The baby looks just like you," her sister-in-law, Sara, said, her eyes misty. "I can't wait to introduce him to his little cousins. Cowboy Joe is watching them right now."

Daisy smiled. Cowboy Joe was the grizzled sixty-two-year-old cook at the guest ranch cafeteria. He adored babies.

Noah put his arm around his wife, and they gazed at the baby. "Welcome to the family, Tony Lincoln Dawson," he said to his nephew. "You're gonna be spoiled rotten."

Daisy grinned. She felt so lucky that her baby would have five incredible uncles, one amazing aunt and two instant baby cousins. Sara had five-month-old twins, Annabel and Chance. Sara's husband had died just a couple months after she'd given birth to twins, only one of whom had survived—supposedly. Within a half hour of the birth, Sara's twisted husband had actually left frail newborn Annabel on Noah Dawson's doorstep after telling Sara the girl twin had died. But the truth had come out seven weeks later, and Sara and her daughter had been reunited. Noah, who for all that time had taken care of Annabel on his own, thinking she was his baby—per the false, anonymous note left with her—had never looked so happy than on his wedding day, when he, Sara and the twins became a forever family.

Ford stepped back in the room, pocketing his phone. "Harrison McCord is a successful businessman—mergers and acquisitions—in Prairie City. Owns his own firm. Clean record. On local charitable boards. Highly regarded. From basic reports, a top-notch guy."

"Well, he did deliver Tony and ruin a really expensive-looking dress shirt," Daisy said with a grin. "So that's not a *total* surprise."

"He lied about not having a middle name, by the way," Ford added. "It's Leo."

"*L* for Leo!" Daisy said. "Turns out Harrison Leo McCord got a piece of the middle-name honoring whether he liked it or not."

"Probably just didn't want a fuss made over what he did," Rex said. "Likely he doesn't think he did anything anyone else wouldn't have done."

Except Harrison was the only person around. And he had come to her rescue. So that was all she knew.

"Still worth keeping an eye on," Axel put in, and Daisy caught Ford and Noah nodding.

She wondered what was behind Harrison's mysterious behavior. Still, when a nurse came in to check her vitals and bring Tony to the nursery, she forced herself to stop thinking about her impromptu birth partner so she could catch a much-needed nap. But between wishing she could have Tony back in her arms and wondering about Harrison McCord, she was wide-awake.

With visiting hours at the Gentle Winds hospice about to end, Harrison sat at the bedside of ninety-four-year-old Mo Burns, an over-bed table between them holding a deck of cards, Mo's favorite candy—sour jelly beans—and a full house. Mo had beaten Harrison at poker again.

"Gotcha, kid," Mo exclaimed in his whispery voice, his filmy blue eyes beaming with pride.

Harrison had been volunteering at Gentle Winds, where his aunt was a patient just down the hall, ever since Lolly McCord had moved in ten days ago. Lolly had stage-four cancer, caught too late to do anything, and she was often very tired. Harrison liked to be close by to his only relative, so he'd asked about volunteering, and every day, before or after he visited his aunt, he'd spend an hour or so with a few different patients, reading to them, talking sports, playing cards and often just listening to a lifetime of memories. Eighty-eight-year-old Clyde Monroe liked to talk politics, so Harrison read to him from the *Converse County Gazette* about national and local happenings. Danielle Panowsky loved reading true-crime books but couldn't see the tiny type anymore and couldn't stand e-readers or earphones, so Harrison found her a few great crime podcasts they could listen to together. And Mo liked poker and winning, so Harrison mostly let the sweet man win. But today, Harrison hadn't even had to ignore his good cards. His mind was not on the game.

"How's your aunt feeling today?" Mo asked, picking up his cards.

"Lolly was sleeping when I arrived. I'll check in on her in a little while."

Mo nodded. "You're a good nephew. I've got so many nieces and nephews and grands and great-grands I can't keep their names straight, but I love when they come see their old great-uncle Moey. They always bring me my favorite beef jerky. I can't chew it, but I love the smell of it."

Harrison laughed. He adored Mo. And he'd met quite a few of Mo's boisterous, large clan, a few always popping in every day. Harrison had figured he'd be paired with patients who didn't get many visitors, but he was assigned to anyone who'd filled out a form requesting volunteer visitors—or their families had. For Mo, the more the merrier.

Harrison's aunt Lolly wasn't the type to want someone sitting in the chair beside her and reading from *Anne of Green Gables*, her favorite novel. Lolly had always been private and a keep-to-herself kind of person. Harrison was a little too much like that, but he was working on it. He'd lost his father a couple weeks ago, and when the grief had grabbed him particularly hard one night and he'd gone for a drive and passed a health club, he'd gone in, signed up for membership, and taken out his frustrations on the treadmill and punching bag and weights, and he'd felt a lot better when he'd left. It was also good to be around people who didn't know him, unlike at work, where the looks of sympathy over his dad had gotten hard instead of comforting.

"You seem upset to me, buddy boy," Mo said. "Spill the beans. Back in the day, people told me all their troubles. I shoulda charged ten bucks a trouble."

Harrison smiled. "I'm all right." *Sort of. Except for losing my dad. And now having to say this hard goodbye to my aunt.* And then there was the matter of Daisy Dawson.

All the Dawsons, really. But particularly her now.

"Guess what?" Harrison said. "I helped deliver a baby on the side of the road earlier today." He felt himself smiling, the marvel coming into his face. "Isn't that something? A boy."

He thought of Daisy's big blue eyes. Little Tony wrapped in Harrison's shirt. Daisy wanting to give Tony his middle initial as a way to thank him.

He'd practically run out of her room after that. But he'd have to face her tomorrow. With some news she wasn't going to like.

"I did that once," Mo said, his eyes lighting up. "Hand to God. Lady went into labor right in front of me while I was showing a house. Did I tell you I used to be a real estate agent? It was just the two of us, and wham, the baby was coming. The ambulance got there a minute after I helped deliver the baby. I didn't know what the hell I was doing."

Harrison stared at him. "Are you serious? That *just* happened to me. How can it be this common?"

"Hey, we're a couple of uncommon dudes," Mo said. "Baby was a girl and squawking her head off."

Harrison laughed. "So what happened?"

"Well, a couple days later, the lady's husband came to see me and tried to give me a hundred bucks and a cigar. I took the cigar and told him it was something anyone would do. But I'll tell you,

I did feel like a hero. I told that story for months until my brother told me to shut up already."

Harrison smiled. "I felt like a hero, too." But then his smile faded as he realized he was the opposite of a hero. He'd helped bring little Tony Dawson into the world—but was about to take something away from Daisy.

Her family ranch.

Which was really *his* family's ranch.

How the hell was he going to tell her?

Every time he thought, *Why did I have to be at the right place at the right time*, he'd then realize—*thank God I was*. He couldn't imagine that beautiful woman, so full of life, literally, giving birth alone on a stretch of rural road. Yes, getting rather intimate with Daisy Dawson had thrown a monkey wrench into things, but he'd come to the Dawson Family Guest Ranch to right a wrong, and he would. Whether he'd delivered Daisy's baby or not. Whether he felt a connection to her—and that tiny baby—or not.

That's neither here nor there, he forced himself to think, recalling his father's favorite line when someone would try to inject emotion into business. Business was business. Signed documents mattered. The Dawson Family Guest Ranch was rightfully his father's property, and now his. And he'd get it back in the name of his father.

And for Lolly—there was a long story there that he didn't want to think about. Not with his aunt five doors down, barely able to consume even clear soups in the past couple of days. He had a lifetime of wonderful memories of family holidays and special celebrations with his dad and Lolly, and he'd hold on to those.

Mo's eyes started to flutter closed, so Harrison packed up the cards and moved the table and jelly beans. He patted sweet Mo's hand.

"I'll see you tomorrow, friend," he told Mo.

Daisy had mentioned she'd be getting discharged tomorrow afternoon. Harrison would stop by the main house at the ranch in the early evening and explain the situation. Who he really was. Why he was there. What the law said. He felt terrible about it, given the new circumstances, but he had to stop seeing Tony Dawson's little fingers and button nose and bow lips—and Daisy Dawson's big blue eyes, so full of *thank you* that he couldn't bear it.

You're righting a wrong, he reminded himself. *Just focus on that. Do what you have to do and leave and you'll never have to see those big blue eyes again.* He'd never stop thinking about them, though.

How in the world was he going to tell Daisy he was taking away her home and family business?

Tony's home and family business? A beautiful newborn he'd helped deliver.

Suddenly, *that's neither here nor there* wasn't working for him. Not one bit.

Chapter Three

"So I brought you some stuff you'll *really* need," Sara said with a smile, plopping into the chair beside Daisy's hospital bed. She had a big red tote bag on her lap.

Daisy grinned and sat up, baby Tony sleeping nestled against her chest. The Dawson crew had left a few hours ago, and since visiting hours were ending in about a half hour, Daisy hadn't expected to see any of them until tomorrow, when Noah and Sara would come pick up her and Tony to bring them home. She should have known her BFF would be back.

Sara pulled out three books. "Okay, you might

not exactly have time to read. But if you do, you'll want these. One," she said, holding up a hardcover with "*New York Times* bestseller" atop it. "*Motherhood for Total Beginners: Your Guide to Fusspots, Colicky Screamers, Nonnappers, Binky-Spitter-Outters, Diaper Rash and a Total Lack of Help*."

Daisy laughed. "That last bit clinches it as definitely the read for me, since I'll be on my own." A second ago she'd been smiling, but the moment the words were out of her mouth, she frowned, that vague fear that sometimes gripped her now hanging on tight. She'd expected to be coparenting. With a husband, her baby's father. Instead, she'd be a single mother. Alone, alone, alone.

"Hey," Sara said, giving Daisy's hand a squeeze. "You've got me 24/7 a quarter mile away. Even if I'm in the middle of breaking up an argument between the goats or dealing with a guest issue, I'll come running. You know that, right? So will Noah."

She did know that. And she loved Sara and Noah for it. Having her family's support made everything about single motherhood a lot less scary. "I don't know what I'd do without you two."

Sara smiled and held up the next book. "*Your Baby's Development by Month*," she read. "This one is a little more boring but very informative. My own copy is already full of Post-its. Basically what to expect. Don't read ahead or you might get scared. Teething?" Sara mock shivered. "That's next for us." She held up the third book, a hard-cover with pretty illustrations on the front. "This one is a baby book." She flipped a few pages. There were pages to write down baby's first word, laugh, step. "Every time Tony has a first, you can record it, and there are spaces for accompanying photos. Annabel's and Chance's baby books are full of blurry shots of them having their first spoonfuls of pureed peaches."

Daisy laughed. "I love these, Sara. And thank you."

Sara reached into the bag and pulled out a huge bag of lemon drops, which were Daisy's favorite candy, and waved it. "Also in here? Everything a new mother needs—from nipple cream to a sitz bath to Extra-Strength Tylenol to this coupon indicating that Noah and I hired a cleaning service to come every other week for a few months."

Daisy's eyes misted. "I could not love you more."

"Hey, that's what besties are for. Plus you're lucky that I'm also your sister-in-law, so you get the BFF love and the family treatment."

"Thank you, Sara. Seriously." She bit her lip and eyed the scary stuff in the tote bag. She'd read about those items but had forced them from her mind, so she hadn't bought them. She was grate-

ful to know she'd have them stored in the bathroom when she'd need them. "I wonder what it'll
be like, being home with him on my own. Doing
this alone. I mean, I know I have you and Noah.
But there's no dad, Sara. You went through that. I
know you know it's scary."

"It is scary," Sara said. "But just like I knew I'd
be all right, you know you'll be all right. You do
what you gotta do. You accept support. You say
yes to every offer of help. You ask for help when
you need it. You learn on the job. And the job
is everything, Daize—motherhood. And motherhood is truly instinctive. The incredible love you
feel for Tony, that love you've never felt before in
your entire life before you held him? That guides
everything. Everything else you look up in these
books or google it. Like sudden bumpy rashes on
Tony's chest or a barking cough."

Daisy felt instantly better. Yeah—Sara was
right. Daisy had felt an instinctive burst of love,
protectiveness, commitment, everything the moment Harrison McCord had placed her newborn
baby boy on her chest. She'd be a good mother—
she knew she would be. And for all the scary stuff
that would come up, she'd ask Sara, who had several months of experience on her, or she'd hit the
laptop.

She breathed a sigh of relief. "Gimme a lemon drop."

Sara grinned and handed over the bag, two pounds' worth and tied with a red wire bow. A few minutes later, a nurse popped her head in and pointed at her watch. Visiting hours were over for the day. Sara gathered her stuff, assured Daisy she and Noah would be back tomorrow afternoon to bring her and Tony home to the ranch, and then it was just Daisy and her newborn.

Daisy was going to be just fine. She and baby Tony were a team, a family. And she had a big support system. Maybe even a new friend, the mystery man guest in Cabin No. 1 who'd helped bring Tony into the world. She wondered why he'd left so suddenly earlier. Maybe the idea of giving Tony his middle initial was overwhelming for him. After all, he was practically a stranger.

A stranger who'd shared the most intimate, most beautiful event of her life with her.

Hopefully he wasn't expecting his fancy blue dress shirt back. Daisy had a feeling he'd be happy never to see it again. But she would have it cleaned and save it for always. She'd never forget what Harrison McCord had done for her.

"I do wonder what our rescuer is up to," she said to a still-sleeping Tony. "Maybe he just likes coming to dude ranches, staying alone in a cabin meant for four and not partaking in a single activity." She smiled. "That's the thing, Tone. Could be any reason. A million reasons. Maybe he recently lost his parents and they took him to a guest ranch as a kid and he wanted to soak up the memories. Maybe they even took him to the Dawson ranch. You know, I'll bet it's something like that."

Tony's eyes fluttered open as if he agreed.

"I love you, Tony bear. I might be your only parent, but I promise you I'll do the best job I possibly can. We've got this."

Tony's eyes closed again as if he also agreed with that, as if he felt one hundred percent safe with his single mother. Daisy's heart almost burst with happiness and relief.

Late the next afternoon, Daisy stood in the farmhouse nursery with Noah and Sara and gasped as she looked around. She gently put down Tony's infant carrier and unbuckled him, carefully cradling him along her arm as she stepped around the room. The nursery sure looked different than it had a day and a half ago. She'd had the basics of the room set up for a couple months now—the crib, the dresser with its changing pad, the glider—all gifts from Noah a few days after she'd told him she was pregnant. But now there were surprises everywhere. In one corner was an adorable plush child's chair in the shape of a teddy bear for Tony to grow into. And someone had stenciled the wall facing the crib with the moon and stars. Tony's name was also stenciled on his crib, which was Sara's handiwork. And there were stacks of gifts in one corner that she knew were baby clothes and blankets and burp cloths. She wouldn't have to buy anything for Tony for a long time.

"Ford and Rex did the moon and stars," Noah said. "For novice stencilers who had to read the instructions twice *and* watch a tutorial, they did a great job."

"And Zeke and Axel hit up BabyLand and bought that adorable polka-dot rug and the yellow floor lamp," Sara added. "I didn't even go with them to make sure they didn't buy anything weird or clashing, and what they picked out is absolutely perfect."

The room was so cozy and sweet. "You guys are going to make me cry," Daisy managed to say around the lump in her throat as she surveyed the nursery. She used her free hand to swipe under her eyes.

She couldn't say she and her brothers were close—well, except for Noah these days—but they were always there for her. And they'd all been there to meet Tony the day he was born. That was the one lucky thing to come out of her nonwedding—her whole family had already been at the ranch.

This place had always held bad memories for all the siblings, but after inheriting the ranch from their father, they'd all invested in rebuilding and renovating and reopening the Dawson Family Guest Ranch. Noah had done the lion's share on his own; Daisy had been too pregnant to help much when she'd arrived a few months ago, and the four other Dawsons couldn't get away from the ranch fast enough.

Ford had once said hell would freeze over before he'd come back here, a sentiment shared by the other three brothers as well, but Ford, Rex, Axel and Zeke had surprised Noah and Daisy at the grand opening this past Memorial Day weekend. And now Axel was staying at the ranch for a bit. That meant three out of six Dawsons at the ranch at the same time. It was a start. And Daisy was going to run with it.

The Dawson Family Guest Ranch was a completely different place than it had been, beautifully renovated as a modern-rustic dude ranch in the Wyoming wilderness, and being here didn't whip up bad memories for the brothers as they'd expected because of the changes. They still didn't want to be here, though. But it was a good sign that they'd come visit, and Daisy could put her master plan into work on them: finding them love so they'd stay. The thought of having all Tony's uncles in his life on a regular basis, not just a visit at major holidays, made her so happy she could burst. She just had to change their minds about the place in general. Noah had done such a good job with the renovations that the ranch didn't remind them of home anymore at all. A good thing *and* a bad thing.

Noah grinned. "There's more in the living room. A baby swing that plays five different lullabies. A huge basket set up with everything you might need while you're downstairs, from diapers and wipes to pacifiers to burp cloths and a change of clothes. The six-foot-tall giraffe in the corner is from Rex—he had to head home on some emergency business at work."

She smiled at the giant giraffe. "He called me this morning to say goodbye. Ford and Zeke, too."

"Axel is doing my rounds for me," Noah added. "He called me while riding fence and said he took to the routine immediately, remembered everything he'd learned as a kid. It's good to have him back, even just temporarily."

Daisy nodded. It sure was. She did wonder what had gone down to cause Axel's enforced R&R from his search-and-rescue team. He worked primarily in Badger Mountain State Park, about a half hour away, where Daisy herself had once gotten lost on a typically disastrous family trip. He'd tell her and Noah when he was ready, if he ever was. Axel was pretty private. In the meantime, she would distract him with just the right possible romantic interest. She had someone in mind already—two someones, actually, both of whom had been guests at her nonwedding.

She looked around the nursery, her heart bursting. "I love you guys," she said, her eyes misting. She gazed down at Tony, napping away, his bow lips quirking. Her family hadn't let her feel like she'd lost anything with Jacob's abandonment. And last night, during the times she'd actually been alone in the hospital without a nurse in her room for this or that reason, she'd only had to look at Tony or think about him if he were in the nursery, and she felt so filled up it was insane.

"Hungry?" Sara asked. "I stocked your fridge and freezer with all your favorites. You won't need to go grocery shopping till Christmas."

She wrapped her sister-in-law in a one-arm hug. "You're the best." She turned to her siblings. "You're all the best. Thank you for everything. You've outdone yourself. Now go to work. I've got this. I'm just gonna revel in being home and not in the hospital. Since Tony's napping, I'll try to also."

There were hugs, and then Daisy was alone in the house. For months she'd decorated this nursery, bursting with excitement for the day she'd come home with her baby. And here that day was. Between that and the way her family had rallied around her, she really did feel filled up.

She certainly hadn't expected the house would still be so quiet, given the baby, who was now in the crib. He'd transferred without a peep. *May it always be so easy*, she thought with a grin, knowing that would never be the case. She stood looking at him, his chest rising and falling, one little arm up by his ear in a fist. *Welcome home, my sweet Tony bear.* She could barely drag herself away, but she was yawning herself and realized she'd better squeeze in that nap.

She had a monitor set up on her bedside table and cranked it up, then slid into bed with a satisfied *ahhh*. She did sleep for about twenty minutes and woke up kind of groggy and out of it. Tony was still magically sleeping, so she headed downstairs for a cup of coffee, and even though it was decaf, the brew faked her brain into waking up. She responded to texts from her family, who sent her the photos of Tony and her they'd taken that morning, and then the crying began.

Ridiculously thrilled, Daisy raced from the kitchen upstairs into the nursery and scooped up her son and brought him over to the glider to nurse him. When he was finished, she stood up and gave him gentle pats until he burped, and then she changed him, marveling at how beautiful he was. She was a bundle of nerves about whether she was doing everything the right way, but Tony seemed content, so that had to be the guidepost. "How about the grand tour?" she asked. "Did you know I grew up in this house?"

The doorbell rang. The grand tour would have to wait. She wondered who could be visiting, though. Her brothers or Sara would text her before just ringing the bell. And guests of the ranch were always informed upon arrival that the farmhouse on the hill was the family home. With Tony nestled securely in her arms, she walked very carefully downstairs and headed to the door.

She pulled back the filmy white curtain at the door. Harrison McCord.

What was he doing here?

Top-notch or not, and holding another gift for Tony or not—this time a long, floppy yellow bunny—and very attractive or not, with his tousle of dirty-blond hair and green eyes, he was hiding something. Daisy had no idea if it was something completely innocuous, but he was *definitely* hiding something. He seemed too…intense at the moment not to be.

"I'm sorry for just dropping by," Harrison said.

"But I do need to talk to you. And to your brother, the foreman, as well."

Okay, this was unexpected. What was going on?

She lifted her chin and narrowed her eyes at him and then at the manila envelope he held in his other hand. He wanted to talk to them both? "I was the guest relations manager until just last week, so I'm your guy—gal—" She grimaced. "I'm a good contact if you're having any issues with your stay, is what I mean."

"It's nothing like that," he said. "I'd really like to talk to you both—together."

Hmm. What was this about? "Well, Noah is pretty busy right at the moment. He was here a couple hours ago, but he just texted me he's dealing with our runaway goat, Hermione. Treated like gold but takes off every chance she gets."

He attempted a half smile, but it was so awkward that an alarm bell went off. Something was wrong here.

"Can I come in?" he asked, practically strangling the yellow bunny, whose head and long ears were sticking out of the small gift bag in his left hand.

Daisy reluctantly stepped aside, and he walked in. She closed the screen door behind her.

"Let's go sit in the living room. I have decaf coffee, lemonade, tomato juice, orange juice, cranberry juice. I like juice, obviously," she added, then rolled her eyes at herself for rambling out of sheer nerves.

"Cranberry juice sounds good," he said. "But let me get it. You've got Tony."

"I'll put him in the bassinet," she said, carefully lowering the baby down.

She noticed Harrison staring at Tony, his expression...what? Like a mix of apology and resolve. Just what did he have to talk to her about? Something that also concerned Noah.

She gestured at the gray sectional, and he sat down on one end, looking around the room. The stone fireplace with all the photos, particularly. He got up and walked over to them. He looked at one in particular, of her grandparents standing in front of the big banner on the gates of the Dawson Family Guest Ranch. "Opening day fifty-two years ago," he read from the banner. He then picked up the next photo. It was of the Dawson siblings in the same spot, Memorial Day weekend—similar banner, but this one said Grand *Re*opening. "Opening day two months ago," he added, putting the photo back.

"Noah really did wonders with the place," she said. "I came back only a couple months before we reopened. This was really his baby. But it became my refuge when I had nowhere else to go when

Jacob dumped me the first time around, back when I lived in Cheyenne." Oh cripes, she thought, embarrassed she'd said all that. "Hormones. Making me spill my guts like a crazy person."

He stared at her as if taking in everything she'd said. "I didn't realize Tony's father had a second chance. That makes it even worse."

Didn't she know it. "I usually abide by the 'once burned, twice shy' saying. But I wanted to try for the baby's sake." Why was she telling this man her personal life details? He was here to talk to her about something…serious, from the looks of him. *Get his cranberry juice and let him get on with it.*

"I'll be right back. You'll keep an eye on Tony?" she asked.

His eyes widened just enough for her to catch it. He was either surprised she'd ask him such a thing because he'd never been around babies much, or he was about to spring some bad news on her, like that he'd burned down his cabin or something. "Uh, okay," he said, shifting a bit closer to the edge of the sofa where Tony lay in his bassinet.

She came back with two glasses of cranberry juice and a plate of Cowboy Joe's coconut fudge cookies, which he'd sent to the main house this morning with Noah. Cowboy Joe had a big enough workload, but he'd kept her cravings satisfied with his delicious homemade fare and snacks. Sometimes treats she didn't even know she wanted until there they were, on a plate, beckoning her. She wasn't pregnant anymore, but she craved these cookies big-time.

She sat down across from the sofa on the love seat, where she could directly see Harrison and the baby. "So what's this about?" she asked. "Is something wrong? Are you leaving us a terrible review on TripAdvisor or something?"

He seemed so caught off guard that he smiled for a second, but then it faded. "I'm just going to come right out with this, Daisy. The Dawson Family Guest Ranch doesn't rightfully belong to your family. It belongs to mine."

She stared at him. "What on earth are you talking about? How could this place possibly belong to your family?"

"Your father, Bo Dawson, signed over ownership of the ranch to my father ten years ago." He reached for the manila envelope he'd settled on his lap, opened it and pulled out a folded, yellowing square napkin, the kind servers set down on your table before plunking your beer on top of it. "The proof," he said and reached over the coffee table to hand the napkin to her.

What the hell is this? she wondered, taking the napkin. Staring back at her was her father's unmistakable scrawl in black pen. It was dated

June 15 ten years ago. *I lost the bet and transfer ownership of the Dawson Family Guest Ranch to Eric McCord.*

Daisy gasped. Her father had bet the ranch?

"This is some drunken bar thing," she said. "It wouldn't hold up in a court of law." She eyed the napkin again, her stomach churning suddenly, and handed it back to him, wanting it away from her as quickly as possible. Her father had drunk way too much, particularly the last couple of years before his death. She had no doubt he was five sheets to the wind when he'd bet the ranch. And left signed proof.

"I've consulted two attorneys who assure me it will hold up," Harrison said, so seriously that she sat straight up.

Daisy lifted her chin. "I think I should get my brothers over here before we say more. They should be in this conversation. Only Noah and Axel are still here. Ford, Rex and Zeke left early this morning."

Harrison nodded.

She stared at him, half scared, half hating his guts, and then grabbed her phone off the coffee table. She texted Noah.

Emergency. Harrison McCord says the ranch is his family's, that Dad signed it over. Has napkin proof. He's in the farmhouse. Find Axel and hurry!

Be right there. Texting Axel, Noah responded.

Daisy sat still as a board, hands in her lap, clasping and unclasping. Harrison did the same. They looked everywhere but at each other.

A few minutes later, Noah stormed in, Axel right behind him. Harrison stood up, the envelope in his hand.

"What the hell is this?" Noah said. "Napkin proof? What?"

Harrison gave the envelope to Noah, who opened it and pulled out the napkin. Daisy waited for shock to register and his muscles to bunch, and that's exactly what happened.

"This won't hold up in court," Noah said, passing the napkin to Axel. "Clearly drunken nonsense."

Daisy shivered, despite the eighty-one-degree temperature. "I said the same thing. He said two attorneys assured him it *would*."

"What's the story behind this?" Axel asked Harrison after reading the napkin for himself and putting it back in the envelope.

Harrison practically snatched back the envelope and held on to it.

"Let's all sit," Daisy said.

They sat, not taking their eyes off Harrison Mc-Cord.

Harrison picked up his cranberry juice, which

Daisy now wanted to pour over his head. How dare he drink her juice after threatening to take away their family business? She watched him take a long sip.

"On his deathbed two weeks ago, my father told me that ten years ago, he got into a fight with a Bo Dawson to defend the honor of his sister, my aunt Lolly, who Bo was three-timing. Bo apparently said that his face was too good-looking to risk getting rearranged and he'd challenge my dad to a poker game. If my dad won, then he could beat Bo to pulp. But if Bo won, my dad would have to leave him be forever."

Oh Lord. That did sound like her father. "Where does the napkin come in?"

"At the bar where they were going to play in a back room, Bo started flirting like crazy with the waitress, who wore a wedding ring. My dad got even angrier at how Bo used and abused people that he demanded Bo up the stakes or he'd bash his face in right there. Because Bo had pissed off most guys around, no one was going to come to his rescue."

"So our dad bet his ranch?" Noah asked. "The family ranch his parents built from nothing? No way."

"Your father told my dad he owned his family's very popular dude ranch in Bear Ridge. My dad had heard of the place, so he said fine, put it in writing and we'll play for it. Your dad did." He held up the envelope."

"And our dad lost," Axel finished, shaking his head.

Harrison nodded. "The ranch, therefore, belongs to my family."

"Now, wait a minute," Daisy snapped, standing up and putting her hands on her hips. "It most certainly does not! A drunkenly scrawled napkin from ten years ago? Your own father could have written that. My dad never mentioned a lost bet and signing over the ranch. That napkin isn't proof of anything."

"Except it's your dad's handwriting," Harrison said. "I did some investigating."

Daisy gasped. "How dare you! Lurking around, spying on our history."

Noah and Axel both dropped down hard on chairs with pent-up breaths.

"It's not personal," Harrison said. "It's just business. And this is the business I'm in. Mergers and acquisitions. Your father signed over ownership, but when my dad discovered the place was a falling-down mess, he didn't collect. I'm here to do just that."

Steam was coming out of Daisy's ears. "Oh, right, suddenly after Noah rebuilds the place and it opens to rave reviews! If you think you're taking the Dawson Family Guest Ranch from us, you have another think coming, mister." She stuck her arm out, finger pointing at the front door. "Get out of my house!"

Harrison had the gall to look hurt. "I just found out about the bet and the napkin a couple weeks ago when my father died. My aunt Lolly rarely talks about her private life, but my father filled me in on how Bo destroyed her faith in men and love and romance. She never dated again after the way he treated her. She just gave up. Now she's dying in a hospice in Prairie City all alone."

For a moment, all Daisy heard was that his father had passed away two weeks ago and now his aunt was dying alone in Prairie City, which was the big town that bordered Bear Ridge. Daisy had lost her mom young and her dad last Christmas. Her heart went out to him. Until she remembered why he was here.

"I'm sorry about the loss of your dad," she said. "And about your aunt. But the Dawson Family Guest Ranch belongs to *us*." She crossed her arms over her chest.

"I'm sorry, too, but again, a deal is a deal," Harrison said. "The ranch belongs to the McCords in my father's and aunt's dual honor. So I will see you in court."

Daisy gasped. He was taking them to court? He couldn't be serious!

"I'd like you to leave," she shouted, causing Tony's eyes to slowly open. The baby scrunched up his face and let out a cry.

Harrison eyed Tony, then lit out of the house fast.

"And take your stupid bunny with you," Daisy yelped, throwing it after him.

It landed in front of the door that Harrison had just closed behind him.

"Tell me that idiotic napkin won't hold up in court," Daisy said, looking between Noah and Axel.

Her brothers looked at each other, then at her.

"It very well could," Noah said. "Social gambling is legal here—in private homes and bars. The napkin is dated, very clear in content and signed."

Axel sighed. "We'll get our own lawyer. We'll fight this with everything we've got."

Damn right, they would. This ranch was their legacy. Their children's future. No one was taking it away.

She looked at Tony. Tony Lincoln Dawson. Just yesterday she'd been tickled to discover that Harrison's middle name started with *L* and that she'd chosen a middle name with that initial. Well, from here on in, that *L only* stood for her mother's name, Leah. Harrison and his middle name could go jump in a lake.

Chapter Four

Harrison wished he had the magic words to make Aunt Lolly feel more at peace. She'd been at the Gentle Winds hospice for ten days, her condition worsening, he believed, by losing her beloved only sibling and attending the funeral, which had been hard on her. He knew his visits made her happy, and if she was asleep during his visit, he always left her a cheerful greeting card from the stack he'd bought in the gift shop.

Dear Aunt Lolly, I sat with you till they kicked me out when visiting hours ended. I love you. See you tomorrow. Your nephew, Harry.

He wasn't a Harry, had never been a Harry with anyone but Aunt Lolly. She always called him that when they were together. Now, as he sat at her bedside, a hard knot of grief formed in his chest all over again. Lolly was napping, as she often was these days. And as he was sitting there, staring up at the leaf-patterned ceiling tiles that his aunt had admired the day she'd arrived, Daisy Dawson's pretty, glowy face came to mind. And all that had gone down at her house an hour ago.

He'd left feeling like the biggest jerk in Wyoming. But as he looked over at his frail aunt, alone except for him, the tension in his shoulders started to loosen, his head cleared and his conscience wasn't poking at him. Being with Aunt Lolly reinforced what he was doing and why. The Dawson Family Guest Ranch belonged to his father. In honor of Lolly McCord.

Harrison visited his aunt every day before his daily volunteer shifts. In fact, he'd been headed to the hospice yesterday when he'd come across Daisy in labor. He'd stopped in to see Lolly after he'd visited Daisy and Tony in the hospital, grateful that Lolly had been asleep since he'd been so wound up. Daisy had wanted to give her son his middle initial. Because she'd had no clue about the bombshell he'd been about to drop.

And now had.

He leaned his head back. What a mess.

He was glad Lolly was sleeping right now, since he was so distracted he wouldn't be fully present. Then again, when Lolly wasn't sleeping, she said very little. She liked to keep the conversation light, about the weather and how nice her nurses were, particularly Patricia with the "lovely bright red hair" and how she just loved the butterscotch pudding and Patricia made sure she had that for dessert every night. And she loved talking about her younger brother, Eric—Harrison's dad—eight years her junior and her hero. Eric had always adored his big sister.

Now, Daisy Dawson's *Get out of my house* ringing in his head, he wished Lolly would wake up so he could focus on his aunt instead of the shock in Daisy's pretty blue eyes. She'd almost looked betrayed, he supposed, because of what they'd gone through together.

He shook his head. This wasn't about Daisy. Taking the ranch was about his father and Lolly. Period. Nothing against the Dawsons. Well, maybe against one Dawson—Daisy's father.

Lolly might not be one to talk about her personal life, but Harrison's dad had told him all about how that rat bastard Bo Dawson had destroyed Lolly's faith in men and love, and she'd just "given up" after discovering he was not only cheating on her with a good friend of hers, but with another woman, too. Apparently, Bo had told Lolly he was saving up for an engagement ring for her, two carats like she deserved, and at fifty-five and long divorced, with no children, Lolly had truly thought she'd finally met her second chance at love. But that had apparently been Bo Dawson's MO, charming his way into women's hearts, having them foot the bill for their romance until he either dumped them or they caught on.

Harrison had seen a photo of the guy—Lolly had a few of the two of them in the last album she'd made up. Bo Dawson had looked a lot like Pierce Brosnan, way back when. His aunt Lolly had been madly in love, then ended up losing her good friend, her faith in love and a solid chunk of her retirement fund to "spotting" Bo money for this or that she'd never seen again, and clearly the ranch hadn't, either. He'd obviously spent the money he manipulated out of her on other women, drinking and gambling.

And Lolly had never put herself out there again. Fifty-five had been way too young to give up on happiness, on a life partner with whom to grow old, and now Lolly was sixty-five and had been on her own ever since Bo had betrayed her.

Eric McCord had told him all this in the hospital bed Harrison had set up for his dad at home. Eric hadn't wanted to go to hospice, he'd wanted his son to take care of him in his final days, and Harrison had, delegating a good chunk of work at the firm he owned. His father had shown him the napkin and said that he'd heard the Dawsons reopened their guest ranch and that he wanted Harrison to get it back for Eric and Lolly's honor. Harrison assured him he would.

The few times Harrison had tried to bring up Bo with Lolly in her hospice room, she'd looked uncomfortable and had said she didn't want to talk about bad memories. Harrison's anger at Bo Dawson had ignited every time. That fink Bo had cheated Harrison's dad out of a punch in the face and the ranch he'd signed over to him, and he'd used Lolly and had broken her heart. Hell yeah, Harrison was going to right the wrongs of the past.

He opened up one of the photo albums that Lolly had stacked on the table beside her. Pictures of her childhood, with her brother and their parents and their parents, and dog after dog over the years. Last night, since she'd been asleep, Harrison had looked through an album of when she and his father had been little kids. He couldn't believe the two of them had ever been that young. He couldn't believe *he'd* ever been that young. He felt like a hundred.

And he felt like hell. Telling the Dawsons that he was coming for their ranch was a lot harder when he'd shared one of the most special moments in Daisy Dawson's life with her. Maybe the most special.

And yes, that look on her face as she'd told him to leave. He'd never forget the worry, the sadness, the anger, the betrayal in those beautiful blue eyes. Making baby Tony cry.

He hung his head in his hands. He wished he could right that, too.

I'm doing what I'm supposed to be doing, Lolly, he silently told his aunt. *But doing the right thing rarely feels so wrong.*

It was wrong. And right.

Oh hell. He had to stop that, get out of that mind-set. Taking what rightfully belonged to his family wasn't wrong. His father had agreed to accept the ranch for the bet because he'd *believed* it was fully operational and profitable—not some dilapidated, run-down ghost ranch that hadn't had a guest in years. When Eric McCord had gone to see the property he'd won, the grass had grown wild and there wasn't an animal in sight, not even a stray cat. Bo Dawson was actually living there, in the falling-down foreman's cabin, since half the main house had been destroyed with what looked like a pickup truck running into it, his father had thought. Eric had thought about taking the ranch for the land, but he didn't need the money, and putting money into this wreck of a place? Forget it. So he'd walked away—but held on to the napkin.

Eric McCord had been a wonderful man, true blue, compassionate, kind. Harrison wasn't going to let him down. Or Aunt Lolly. The ranch was rightfully the McCords'.

I'm doing the right thing, he told himself, giving Lolly's hand a gentle squeeze.

And this time when Daisy Dawson's beautiful face and Tony's wispy curls and matching big blue eyes came into mind, he forced down a steel wall.

With her baby in a sling on her chest, Daisy stood with Sara behind the "Help Yourself" table at the back of the ranch's cafeteria. There, guests could always find muffins, cereal bars, fruit and beverages, especially coffee. Daisy and Sara were replenishing the trays and bowls and adding bottled water to the coolers that lined the rear of the table. Well, Sara was doing the replenishing, since Daisy was technically on her maternity leave and not officially on the job for the next six weeks. But she needed to talk to Sara, and she could certainly add more muffins to the case while she let off steam about the Harrison McCord mess.

"I can't believe he's really going to take us to court," Sara whispered, putting chocolate chunk, raspberry and oat bran bars in the big bowl from the cart she'd wheeled over from the kitchen. "How could he? On such flimsy evidence?"

Flimsy evidence was right. Humph. What was real evidence was straight ahead of them in the cafeteria. The happy guests, the hardworking staff, the smooth-running hum of the Dawson Family Guest Ranch. All the guests, except for you-know-who in Cabin No. 1, were here having breakfast.

The Monellos, young, usually lip-locked newlyweds on their honeymoon, had their arms entwined as they fed each other bites of the breakfast special, a western omelet. The Humphreys, who were a little argumentative with each other but seemed to dote on their teenaged son, had the round table with a view of the sheep pasture. Daisy could hear the parents arguing about salt consumption. They were trial lawyers, so perhaps this was just how they operated in daily life. Then there was the mother and daughter duo from Cabin No. 4, who snapped at each other constantly but at least were here together, having their breakfast and laughing over the antics of Hermione and Snape, the goats jumping onto big rocks in the pasture.

And the occupants of Cabin No. 5, a stylish couple from New York City who hadn't brought appropriate footwear for riding or hiking and actually had to go buy sneakers in Prairie City, were looking at the colorful blackboard of the day's activities that hung on the left wall. Daisy heard them excitedly talking about their very first horseback-riding lessons. The family in Cabin No. 6 had checked out early this morning, and a new group was expected this afternoon. All the guests looked happy.

And the guy in Cabin No. 1? Hiding out? Planning a coup today? She wished he were here with everyone else, watching how hard Cowboy Joe and his staff worked on the meals, how much the families—people of all ages—were enjoying the breakfast, what it clearly meant to her and Sara to see this room full again when for so many years it was a run-down nothing overtaken by a family of raccoons.

He couldn't take the ranch from them. Could not.

Daisy liked the way Sara put it: flimsy evidence. "I know. A yellowed cocktail napkin from ten years ago." She rolled her eyes, but then the worry set right back. "Noah and Axel say it could be binding because it's not only dated but signed by my dad, and it's clearly his crazy handwriting with the weird left-leaning all caps."

Sara shook her head, adding two bunches of bananas to a cloth-lined basket. "I heard Noah on FaceTime with Zeke, Rex and Ford last night. They all sounded worried, too, and said if it came to it, they'd hire the best lawyer in the state—a shark to deal with a shark—and Harrison McCord would be sent packing."

Daisy plucked a purple grape off the bunch that Sara put in the big fruit bowl and popped it into her mouth, then another. "What I don't get is how he can even think of trying to take away our family business. That my grandparents started. That Noah rebuilt himself after ten years of ruin. Suddenly the Dawson Family Guest Ranch is open again and a big success, and he's laying claim. I don't think so, jerk face."

"Right?" Sara said. "It's hard to believe that a guy who'd help deliver your baby and visit you in the hospital with that cute teddy bear would be capable of such a thing."

Daisy nodded. "That's just it. It doesn't really make sense. I know he thinks he's doing it for his father's memory and his aunt's honor, and there's some real heavy stuff involved in all that. But the Harrison I got to know briefly seemed so kind and generous. He has such warm eyes. I had such a wonderful feeling about him. And then, wham, he shows up with that stupid napkin, making threats to see us in court."

"He didn't check out of the cabin, by the way," Sara said. "I thought he might hightail it off the ranch and deal with this from where he lives. But he's still here."

"Probably because he thinks the whole place is *his*." Daisy narrowed her eyes. "I'm going to tell him he can't try to take the ranch from us. He's gotten to know us a bit as people and not just as names on a piece of paper. That has to make a difference."

Sara gasped. "Daisy. That's it. That's it exactly!"

"What's it exactly...exactly?"

"Show that man who you are," Sara said. "Who the Dawsons are. What this place means to all of you. To this little dude," she said, leaning over to plunk a kiss on Tony's head, just visible in the sling. "If he has half the heart you think he has, there's no way he'd try to enforce a ridiculous drunken ten-year-old bet that takes away the legacy of the baby he delivered."

Daisy stared at Sara with growing wonder, the truth about what her sister-in-law was saying sinking in more and more. "You're right. Mr. McCord likes deals? Well, I'm about to go make him a deal."

Harrison had arrived at the ranch cafeteria at exactly seven o'clock when it opened for a hot breakfast. He'd had the entire place to himself. The special of the day was a western omelet, which he had along with Cowboy Joe's amazing home

fries and three cups of coffee. The breakfast station also featured eggs, bacon, sausage, bagels,
cold cereals, fruit and various juices. None of the
cafeteria staff gave him the evil eye, which told
him the Dawsons hadn't shared his real reason for
being here with the employees.

He took a long walk after breakfast. At one
point he saw Noah Dawson on a brown-and-white
horse, doing what seemed to be a slow surveil of
the property, and Harrison figured the guy was
making sure everything was in pristine condition
for when the guests got out and about, which didn't
seem to be before seven thirty. The grounds were
immaculate, somehow managing to be rustic and
wild and manicured at the same time. If Noah noticed him walking along the creek, he didn't acknowledge him, which Harrison appreciated. An
argument before 8:00 a.m., even after three cups
of coffee, wasn't appealing.

Harrison had to admit he loved this place. The
grounds, the horses and livestock, the beautiful
red and yellow barns. The well-placed benches and
signposts indicating how far they were from various spots, like the cafeteria or the lodge. Despite
having a not-so-pleasant mission here, he was able
to breathe, to relax—well, when not confronting
any Dawsons. He didn't think about work while
he was here. Or what happened with Bethany, the

woman who'd blindsided him when he thought they were getting serious.

I know how you feel, Aunt Lolly, he thought, reminded of all his dad had revealed about her debacle of a romance with Bo Dawson. Ten years alone, though. And now dying. The idea of spending the rest of his life alone sounded pretty miserable. But so did even thinking about taking a chance on dating.

Daisy Dawson and her round blue eyes came to mind. Her long, wavy, wild honey-brown hair. Baby Tony, who looked just like her and his big chubby cheeks. He smiled, then felt it fade. *You just feel bad about what you had to do. First the woman is stood up at the altar. Then she goes into labor alone. Then she finds out some jerk is going to steal her family's ranch away. A single mother who just had a baby doesn't need that extra stress.*

He didn't pride himself on being "some jerk," but he did believe he was right to take back what should have belonged to his family for the past ten years. The Dawsons didn't seem to know anything about his father's bet or the transfer of ownership, but that was Bo Dawson's fault for not telling them what he'd done. The thing that kept tripping Harrison up was that this didn't feel like business. It was actually personal. All feelings, all emotions. Negative ones.

That, Harrison wasn't used to. He liked the black-and-white of documents with the deal laid out to be signed. That, he understood. He lived his life that way now, staying on point, staying all business. He'd tried letting his guard down with Bethany, a VP at a rival company, and found out she was using him to gain information about a corporation his company was interesting in acquiring.

Maybe Lolly's way was the way. She'd worked as a home-care nurse, had enjoyed her job, loved going to the movies and reading and taking Italian classes. She'd avoided friendships after finding out her own good friend was also dating Bo Dawson. Since she'd given up dating and the idea of marriage, she'd spent her time alone if her brother or nephew weren't around. No more broken hearts, no arguments, no dashed hopes or expectations. Just a simple, quiet life of her patients, family and hobbies.

Except now she was dying—all alone, except for Harrison. No life partner, no one at her bedside. He sighed, kicking at a rock and sending it skittering into a bush.

He'd never claimed to have all the answers.

He headed back to his cabin and was halfway there along the path when he saw Daisy Dawson, a blue sling around her torso, coming toward his cabin from the path leading to the cafeteria. Was she coming to see him? Or would this be a very awkward coincidental encounter?

They both stopped at the fork where the paths met. "Morning," he said. He peered a bit closer at the sling. He could see Tony's yellow-capped head.

"Mr. Businessman who likes deals," she said, her blue eyes flashing. "I have one for you."

"Oh?" he asked.

"Why don't we talk privately in your cabin?"

"Okay," he said and they resumed walking side by side.

"Didn't see you at breakfast," she said. "You missed a great omelet."

"I got there first thing, actually. By the time I left, none of the other guests had come yet. I had the excellent fresh-brewed coffee to myself. And one hell of an omelet and great home fries."

"Oh, well I'm glad you're not holing up in your cabin," she said, eyeing him. "Especially since you paid in advance for a week's stay."

"I don't feel entirely comfortable here now that you and your brothers know why I'm really here, but I was starving. I'll plan on checking out today."

She frowned, which confused him, since he thought she'd be thrilled that he was planning to leave. "Well, I'm glad you experienced Cowboy Joe's incredible home fries. I *craved* those home fries for the last few months of my pregnancy.

Cowboy Joe always put aside three servings for me. Those tiny peppers and onions and burned bits. Yum."

He stared at her. She sure was being…friendly. Chatty.

His cabin came into view, surrounded by trees and wildflowers, the pine hitching post, to the left of the small covered porch, that he'd never made use of. He walked up the three steps to the dark wood cabin with its hunter-green shutters. Two rocking chairs were on the far side of the porch, a small table between them. Flower baskets hung from the railing. Lolly would have loved the place.

He unlocked the door and walked in, the bright, airy open-concept layout welcoming. There was a small kitchenette to the left that opened into a living space. Upstairs were two small bedrooms, a king bed in the bigger room and two twins in the other, and a bathroom between them. The furnishings were comfortable and durable at the same time. A slipcovered sectional sofa, a braided oval rug.

"What can I get you to drink?" he asked.

"I'd love something cold and sweet."

"Ginger ale?"

"Perfect!" she said so amiably that he stared at her again, wondering why she was being so warm. She'd said she had a deal for him, and deals were usually not about warmth and friendliness. At least not in his world.

He headed to the half refrigerator, wondering what she had up her sleeve. Or lack thereof, since she wore a pale yellow sundress with white stitching. She had on a floppy sunhat and flip-flops with lobsters on them. He got two bottles of ginger ale and the muffins that Cowboy Joe had insisted he take back to his room this morning and set them on the wood coffee table.

She was sitting smack-dab in the middle of the sofa. He sat on the L of the sectional, a reasonable distance. "Tony's napping. He's turning out to be a champ at that. I had no idea I'd be so lucky. I even got a two-minute shower this morning. My brother Axel is staying with me, but I'd hate to ask him to babysit just yet. The poor guy is on some kind of enforced R&R from his search-and-rescue team. He works out of Badger Mountain State Park."

He handed her a ginger ale, completely perplexed as to why she was treating him like an old friend instead of the vicious interloper trying to destroy her family. "Enforced?" he repeated.

She shrugged. "He's not talking, not that I blame him. I have a feeling a mission got hairy, you know? All he said was that a toddler went missing for over two hours. He found the little guy. But somewhere in there is a story."

Harrison was riveted. "Does he work with a K-9 partner?"

"Yup. A gorgeous yellow Lab named Dude."

He laughed. "Is Dude a houseguest, too?"

She nodded. "Sure is. I love having a dog around. We never did as kids, since guests could be allergic or the liability of having him get loose. You know."

"I do know. A dog once bit me on the calf. One of those tiny ones, half a foot off the ground. Chomp. That bite hurt for a week."

She smiled. "Not that that's funny," she said on a chuckle. "Broke the skin?"

"Yeah. But the poor lady was so beside herself, sobbing and crying and telling Puddles he was a bad boy that I told her as long as I knew I didn't need rabies shots, we'd just call it a day. Luckily Puddles had on his rabies tag with the current year, so all was well."

She smiled that dazzling smile. "Puddles?" She chuckled, then eyed the plate of muffins. "Ooh, don't mind if do help myself to one of Cowboy Joe's chocolate-chunk masterpieces."

Now he smiled, enjoying watching her savor the bite she took, careful not to drop crumbs on her baby's head.

She sure was easy to talk to. They hadn't gotten to talk much while she was giving birth. Of course. Or in the hospital, since she'd shocked him into hightailing it out of there by wanting to honor his role in that birth and give Tony a middle name using his initial.

"Look, Daisy," he said. "For what it's worth, I am sorry about all this. I mean, the napkin and everything." He *was* sorry.

"Sorry enough to rip it up and forget it ever existed?" she asked, staring at him.

Awk-ward. "Well, no. And I'm sorry about that, too."

"You can stuff your sorries in a sack, mister!" she said with an exaggerated frown, then grinned. "Remember that episode from *Seinfeld*? George Costanza kept saying that when anyone apologized to him and no one knew what the hell it meant." She laughed and bit into the muffin again.

Okay, what was going on here? She should be furious and chucking throw pillows at him. Not talking old *Seinfeld* moments and grinning.

The sling around her torso moved, and a little cry burst out. Daisy adjusted the sling and stood, taking Tony out and holding him against her. "There, there," she said, moving back and forth along the side of the coffee table.

He stared at the baby against her chest. Tony was so little! Harrison had helped bring this tiny human into the world. He still couldn't quite believe it, that it had really happened. She glanced at her watch, and he noticed it had Mickey Mouse in the center. "Almost time for lunch, isn't it, my little darling," she cooed, her gaze warm on the baby. "Tell you what, let me just chat with Harrison for a minute and we'll be on our way. 'Kay, sweets?"

Tony did stop fussing, seemingly content to be in a different position. Daisy sat back down.

"You're so natural at motherhood," he said out of the clear blue sky. "I mean, two days ago, it was just you, and now you have a baby and it's like you've been a mother forever." He wondered if fatherhood would be that way. Not that he'd likely get to experience fatherhood himself considering he was heading for his aunt Lolly's route. No more romance, no more heartache.

"I take that as a very high compliment," she said. "Truth be told, I was scared to death that I'd do everything wrong. But three-quarters of this gig seems to be instinct. The other quarter is online."

He smiled. "Thank God for Google."

"Right?" She grinned and gave Tony a kiss on the head, then shifted her body a bit to face Harrison. She looked him square in the eye. "I mentioned a deal, Harrison. I'd like to make you one."

He was burning with curiosity. "I'm listening."

"Something you said earlier about being uncomfortable here now…that's a perfect segue. I mean, here you are, probably sure we're all making voodoo dolls with your face on them or something that you're planning on leaving three days into your week's stay."

He shivered at the thought of the six Dawsons each poking pins into a little cloth replica of him. "Well, not that exactly. But yes, I assume you all despise me, so I think leaving today is a good idea."

"Then I'm very glad I caught you before you did," she said. "Because my proposition is this. Stay for the days you booked. Five more days. In that time, get to know us. Me, Noah, Axel, Tony. Noah's wife, Sara, who's my best friend, and her baby twins, Annabel and Chance. Meet the horses and the petting zoo animals. Meet the staff. Walk the grounds. Ride the whole length of the creek. Hear our stories of growing up here and wanting to leave something special for the next generation. This little guy and his cousins and his cousins-to-be, if my other four brothers get their romantic lives in order."

He narrowed his eyes at her. "You're asking me to like you and your family so that I won't take away your ranch. That's pure manipulation."

"Yes," she said, gently rubbing Tony's back. "But according to you, this is business. A deal.

Transfer of ownership. A wrong righted. I'm here to tell you, Harrison McCord, that in five days, you will like us so much that you couldn't possibly take us to court."

He stared at her. She couldn't be serious. "Then why on earth would I agree to stay and like you?"

"Because you're a good person," she said. "A fair person. The man who stopped to help a woman in labor on the side of the road, who ruined a perfectly good dress shirt, who visited me in the hospital with that teddy bear, is a kind, generous person. I'm asking that guy to give us a chance to show you who we are so that, yes, you won't want to take our family business away from us."

Oh hell. He should get in his car and zoom out of here. He *already* liked her. And Tony. Five days? No. No way. He needed to leave and honor his father's request to right the wrongs of the past, to honor his father trying to avenge his sister's heart. Lolly was dying. His father was gone.

She stared at him, waiting. For an answer, he supposed. But what the hell was he supposed to say to this crazy plan?

"I wasn't going to resort to this, Harrison, but your hesitation leaves me no choice." She stood up right in front of him.

She was a little too close. Close enough that he could smell her shampoo or perfume. Or maybe it was Tony's baby magic. Either way, it was enveloping him. That and what she was saying.

He had to stay strong.

But suddenly he was sweating. "Resort to what?"

"Saying please. *Please* stay for the rest of the days you booked. Get to know me. Get to know my brothers and everything this ranch was and is now. Give us a chance to change your mind. That's what I'm asking. It's not manipulative if I'm saying it straight out."

He had to give her credit for that one. She was damned smart. And the sincerity on her beautiful face had him all twisted around like a hot pretzel.

Walk out now, he told himself. *Get in your SUV and go. Talk to your lawyer today, get this thing going and that will be that.*

"Please, Harrison," she said again, this time reaching out to touch his arm. "Just give me a chance. It's not manipulation—honestly. It's about changing your mind very openly."

Oh hell.

He glanced away from her hopeful, determined blue eyes and the baby in her arms. The one he'd helped bring into this world.

Blast it to bits. Of course he had to say yes. And anyway, every day when he visited Lolly, his resolve to take the ranch for his family would continue to be reinforced. He let that sink in, shore him up. Yes, so really, this plan of hers was all good. Daisy would feel she was doing what she could to stop him. He'd know he'd see them in court. Sort of win-win for both. Until the end, of course, when *he'd* take what he'd come for.

Tony began to fuss again. Harrison knew she had to get going so she could feed him and change him and all that stuff.

He stood up. "I'd shake your hand if both weren't occupied. You have a deal, Ms. Dawson."

Relief settled on her face. "Thank you. Neither of us will regret this."

"We'll see," he said. "I should warn you, Daisy. I *do* mean to take ownership of the ranch. Liking you people and this place or not. I want to be very clear on that."

She lifted her chin. "Five days," she said.

"Five days," he repeated.

She nodded, did some kind of wizardry with the sling and settled Tony back inside, then extended her hand.

He shook it, the feel of her soft, warm hand in his unexpectedly…charged.

"Let's begin with a tour of the ranch," she said. "You've barely seen the place."

"Okay," he agreed. "A tour of the ranch."

It's one little walk. She'll show you the lodge

Chapter Five

"I'd like to start the grand tour at the main house," Daisy said as they headed up the path. "There's something I want to show you." Yessiree, she was going for the kill. She knew *exactly* where to start.

"What is it?" he asked.

"You'll see." She smiled and patted Tony's back.

Harrison lifted his face up to the sky and closed his eyes for a second, the bright sunshine glinting in his thick blond hair, on his cheek, on his forearms. "Well, it's a nice day for a grand tour."

For a moment she let herself ogle how sexy he was. At just a few days postpartum, the fact that she kept noticing was something. She wondered what it meant. That he was so hot *of course* she would appreciate him on a purely physical level? That she was a bundle of hormones and who knew what craziness they were up to?

Or maybe she couldn't help being attracted on a personal level because he'd come to her rescue when she'd really needed help. She couldn't even imagine what she would have done if he and his fancy Lexus hadn't come driving down that road.

Just keep your head around this man, she ordered herself. She'd learned quite a lesson about her proclivity to act first, think second. Angrily chucking her cell phone out her car window into a bush had been plain stupid. Noah had thankfully found it—and her engagement ring, which she hadn't decided what to do with yet—but way after she'd sorely needed it. She would not be impulsive with the most important parts of her life again. And how she responded to Enemy Hot Stuff here was super important.

"No, *you're* the best, my little schmoopy-pie."

"No, *you* are, my turtle dove."

Giant eye roll. That could only be the Monellos. Daisy had been trying to avoid the twenty-something honeymooning newlyweds—walking, talking, constantly lovey-dovey reminders of her wedding that wasn't. But since Tessa and Thomas were headed right for her and Harrison, there was no escaping them.

Happy couples—fine. Newlywed couples who were so in love that Daisy's teeth ached and her heart clenched—not fine. *Take your unbearable joy elsewhere, people!*

Not that she begrudged them—or anyone—happiness. But the Monellos were now lip-locked and trying to walk at the same time. And managing half-okay. They stopped right in the middle of the path to make out, his hands in her hair, her hands crawling up the back of his T-shirt. They were both tall, slender, dark haired and attractive and wearing matching "safari" wear. The couple resumed walking, kissing every five seconds. They were so googly-eyed for each other that they didn't even notice Daisy and Harrison pass right by them.

Sigh. Daisy was just jealous as all get-out. She herself had felt that way a time or two about a guy. Okay, four times. High school boyfriend. College boyfriend who she thought was serious about her until she found him cheating on her. Two other relationships over the years in Cheyenne, where she'd lived before moving back home to help Noah. One of them had been Jacob, her ex-fiancé. Granted, her ardor had quieted down when she'd realized they weren't exactly right for each other. He was uptight about things she'd never be. She was dead set on things that didn't matter all that much to him. By the time they'd realized they were poorly matched despite their chemistry on other levels, she'd discovered she was pregnant. He'd run for the hills, then come back when she was five months along. Then he'd run again.

And just a few days before that second exodus from her life, Tessa and Thomas had gotten married in the events room of the lodge at the ranch. Right where Daisy's wedding was supposed to take place. The Monellos had hired a wedding planner with her own crew to set up the room, and of course Daisy had found reason to check it all out. She'd been surprised to discover the Monellos hadn't really dolled up the place. Wildflowers were in a rustic centerpiece on each table, and each tablecloth was imprinted with illustrations of horses. Turned out the Monellos were horse crazy, and according to their wedding planner, all they needed to make the wedding amazing was their undying love.

Daisy, nine months pregnant then, had almost tipped over at that one. That was how utterly envious she was. Of the *love* part. That was what Daisy truly wanted, but she'd been going for practical, for working with what *was*. Daisy had been so focused on wedding details the two or three days prior to the big day that she hadn't paid much attention to what Jacob was doing, which was slowly—or perhaps quickly—imploding. That had been how important it was for her to try, to give being a family a real shot, and she'd been willing to sacrifice a certain reality to make it happen. Maybe she should be grateful Jacob had blown that to bits.

Eh, why was she going down this lane? It was all in the past and would never be part of her future. A memory for the keepsake chest she wouldn't open, where all her less-than-happy experiences got filed.

She turned to find the Monellos had stopped again and now Thomas was dipping Tessa for a killer kiss.

"Ever been in love like that?" she asked Harrison, forcing her gaze off the lovebirds.

Harrison glanced over at the newlyweds. "I thought so. But now I'm not so sure."

She tilted her head, hoping he'd elaborate. "Why?"

"Time and space," he said. "Distance. I can see things more clearly now."

"Yeah, me, too." She eyed him as they kept walking. "Got your heart broken?"

He hesitated for a bit, seeming to chew that one

over—if he wanted to say so or not. "I did. Pretty bad, too. I found out I was more a stepping-stone for her than anything."

"Sorry," Daisy said, wondering what the woman who'd won his heart was like. What she looked like. An ambitious businesswoman type in an impressive pantsuit with a great little scarf and gorgeous heels, she figured. The opposite of Daisy Dawson, whose job, even with the semilofty title of guest relations manager, required a staff polo shirt, khakis and sneakers.

"Were you thinking marriage?" she asked. Nosily. She couldn't help it.

More hesitation. He glanced toward the Monellos, now distant figures holding hands. "I guess my feelings never got that far. I always knew something wasn't right between us. I think people know when there's a problem, even if they choose to overlook it or rationalize it. It kept me from going overboard."

And here I was willing to go whole hog. Marry. Take vows. "Do you think it's wrong to overlook your problems or issues for the sake of building a family together? I'm talking about me and Jacob, obviously."

He stopped and looked at her. "Of course I don't think that's wrong. That's different. That's about figuring out how to make something work for a greater good. The baby, a family. You tried, Daisy. Sounds like you were willing to put in the work so that Tony could have his mother and father under one roof, an intact family. You wanted that to happen, and you were willing to give up certain things for it."

She bit her lip, surprised that he understood. "My brother Noah told me a time or two that having sane parents who are happy separately instead of miserable together is just as noble when it came to a baby."

Harrison gave a gentle smile. "He's right, too. You're both right."

She kicked at a pebble. "Well, life happens when you're making plans and all that, or whatever the saying is."

"Nothing truer," he said.

They'd been yakking so much she hadn't even noticed they'd made it up to the farmhouse. It was situated on a rise, slightly out of sight of the rest of the ranch due to the cover of trees, but all guests were notified upon arrival that it was the family house and if the foreman wasn't available in his cabin or by cell phone, they could always come to the main house in an emergency. Her grandparents had always kept a room available to guests in the wake of any trouble—from family fights to plumbing problems. Daisy and Noah did that now, always making sure one room was available.

"Here we are, home sweet home." She stopped in front of the house, admiring it as she always did. Once a sagging, peeling, sad affair with a patchy roof, Noah had renovated it to its original grandeur, had it painted an antique white and the door an interesting shade of blue. The porch had an old-fashioned white wooden swing with a yellow cushion, and there were flowers everywhere. Daisy loved the house now. She loved the idea of raising Tony here. How great was it that Uncle Noah and Aunt Sara were just a quarter mile down the road with Tony's little cousins? And now Axel was right under her roof. Harrison's bombshell had blown every other thought out of her head, but once Daisy got her mind cleared and this craziness about the McCords owning the ranch taken care of, she'd focus on finding Axel true love and a new reason to stay in Bear Ridge. Then she'd work on her other brothers.

"So you and Noah share the house? And now Axel?" Harrison asked as they headed up the porch steps.

"It's just me. Noah lives in the foreman cabin with Sara and the twins—just a quarter mile down that path," she added, gesturing behind them. "Sara grew up there when her dad was foreman. Want to hear something nice about my dad? In his will, he left Sara the raised garden plot her late mother had started years ago. It's in the backyard of the cabin."

"That does sound nice. Sara must have been touched."

Daisy nodded. "She was. My dad didn't have two hundred bucks to his name at the end, but he managed to leave us all priceless stuff in letters."

He glanced at her, curiosity flashing in his green eyes. "Oh yeah? What did he leave you?"

She put her hand to her neck and reached for the necklace she wore under her shirt. She showed him the two rings hanging at the end of the eighteen-inch chain. Both were thin bands of gold, but one had a couple of diamond chips in the center. "My mother's wedding rings. My dad could have sold them so many times over the years but he saved them for me, knowing it would mean a lot to me to have them."

"And he left them to you in his will?" he asked as they walked up the porch steps.

With one hand on Tony's back in the sling, Daisy carefully sat down on the swing and Harrison sat beside her—moving as close to the end as he could, she noticed. "Yup. My mother died when I was eleven. I asked my dad for the rings then, but he put me off, saying I'd lose them, and he'd hang on to them for me. Noah told me not to get my hopes up, that our dad probably sold them already for his drinking and gambling habits. The night he told me that, I snooped in my dad's bedroom and found the rings under his socks. Every time I checked, every first of the month like clockwork, the rings were still there."

"That must have been a relief," Harrison said, his gaze warm on hers for a few seconds.

She nodded, the memories, all she'd felt every time the rings had been there, safe and sound, enveloping her. "More than a relief. My dad had always been a heavy drinker and couldn't seem to stay faithful to his wives. I knew, even at eleven, that he was cheating on my mom because I heard a couple of arguments. I knew the truth, but I still wanted to believe in my dad, you know, that he wasn't…a bad person."

"I can certainly understand that," he said—so gently that she almost burst into tears. Talking about her dad wasn't easy, even with Noah. That Harrison was listening so intently and being kind and empathetic had almost opened the floodgates.

"Finding the rings every time under his gnarly,

threadbare socks gave me back my dad in a way," she continued. "You know? No matter what he'd done, I knew he'd loved me, loved my mother. My mother had always believed he loved her despite being a cruddy husband and father, and I had, too. Finding those rings, month after month, kept me believing that love is real, that the word, the feeling can exist in someone even if their actions aren't exactly showing it. Do I sound nuts?"

He touched her hand for just a moment. "No. Not in the slightest."

She wasn't sure why that buoyed her so much, but it did. "About a year later, when I was twelve, I was arguing about this with Noah, who thought our dad was the worst of the worst, and he said Bo had probably drunkenly forgotten he even *had* the rings. So to prove him wrong, I took a risk."

"What did you do?"

"I decided to remind my dad he had the rings by asking him if I was old enough to be trusted with them now that I was starting middle school. My dad made excuses again, that I'd lose them, maybe when I was older, blah, blah, blah. The next day, the rings were gone from under the socks, and I must have cried for an hour straight."

"I can just imagine how painful that must have

been. Twelve-year-old you with so much faith in your dad."

She glanced at him, surprised again at how he seemed to get her. "I was crushed. Noah felt so bad he'd put it in my head to remind my dad about the rings in the first place that he helped me look again when my dad went out that night. The rings were back. Noah said our dad probably *had* forgotten for a while, then maybe put them in his pocket to sell, then realized he couldn't and put them back. I started checking every week, every Friday, and the rings would always be there."

"I'm glad, Daisy." Harrison looked so serious, so moved by the story that she wanted to scooch over a bit closer to him. She almost wished he'd just put an arm around her. She could use even a quarter of a hug right now. But come on—Harrison McCord was the last person on earth who could comfort her. He cleared his throat as if he'd realized the same, given his mission here, and said, "So you wanted to show me something?"

Why had she thought this was a good idea? Maybe she should forget this part of her brilliant plan, which suddenly seemed a little *too* personal. Just talking about her dad and the rings had her all verklempt. By bringing him inside her home and inviting him deeper into her past, into her family, she'd feel completely vulnerable. Exposed.

Personal is *the plan*, she reminded herself, standing up. *Buck up and get down to business. Personal business.*

"Right this way," she said, gesturing toward the front door.

Uh-oh, Harrison thought once he realized just what Daisy Dawson had planned for him. Two words: home movies. They were on the couch with iced tea and Cowboy Joe's three-berry scones on the coffee table. Tony was dozing in his bassinet beside them. The big-screen TV was straight ahead, now showing Anthony Dawson and his wife, Bess, beaming in front of the Grand Opening sign fifty years ago. The video wasn't preserved all that well, but that added to its charm. Harrison could see the family resemblance; Daisy looked a lot like her grandmother.

"Want to hear something wild? My grandparents, those beautiful, young, smiling people you see right there," she added, pointing at the screen, "they met at a dude ranch when they were teens. Gramps was sixteen and Gram was fifteen. They were both on family vacations. They lived over two hours apart but kept in touch writing letters, and the day Gram turned eighteen they got married. Their dream was to one day open their own guest ranch, and they made that dream come true."

He stared at the screen as Anthony Dawson gave Bess Dawson a kiss, both of them beaming with clear happiness and pride as they held oversize scissors and cut the red ribbon at the gates. He could just imagine them madly in love as teens, in their respective homes wishing they could be together, writing long love letters.

The video cut to the stables, where the Dawsons and two hands were helping a line of children get on ponies. Most of the kids were in cowboy outfits with straw hats like Daisy had.

"See the last kid, the one assuring that little girl that the pony is nice?" Daisy asked, reaching for a scone. "That's my dad. He was about ten then. My grandparents always used to talk about what a help he was as a kid. Showing other kids what to do, telling city slickers there was no reason to fear a horse or worry a sheep would eat them." She bit her lip, a wistful smile on her face. "Feels good to watch these old videos. My brothers and I watched hours of them when my dad died. That's what really spurred us all on to rebuilding the ranch."

Harrison watched the video for a moment. Bo Dawson at various ages, working on the ranch as a kid, a teenager. Bo had a big smile and cracked easy jokes that had kids laughing. At one point in the video, Bess Dawson said, "Now boys, less giggling, more listening to the instructions," and Bo gave the boy he'd been helping the side eye and a grin. The kids clearly adored Bo. He seemed good-natured and easygoing with a bit of troublemaker mixed in.

The video jumped ahead in years, the Dawsons getting on in age, Bo with his arm around three different women at various times—the mothers of his kids—the grandkids running around the ranch. There was Daisy as an adorable youngster sitting in a pen and reading a book to the goats. There weren't many clips of the six Dawson grandchildren together, but Harrison was struck by one— Anthony, Bess, Bo and the six kids sitting around a big table in the dining room of what seemed to be this very house, a cake with lit candles in front of one of the boys, Harrison wasn't sure which, but he seemed like one of the oldest. He figured Daisy and Noah's mom was shooting the video. Must have been nice to have such a big family, even if the kids didn't live together. As an only child without any cousins, Harrison had spent a lot of time alone as a kid.

He stared at the screen, watching the birthday

boy blow out the candles, the kids clapping. Bo Dawson got up and cut the cake, giving the biggest slice to the birthday boy, taking requests for frosting edges or roses (that was Daisy). Bo didn't sit back down until everyone had their slice and their cups of milk refilled. After cake, Bo called out that he had a special present for Ford. The troop scrambled out of their seats, and the video camera followed them outside to where a shiny silver-and-orange mountain bike with twenty-one gears was waiting with a big red bow on the handlebars.

Ford wrapped his arms around his father, and for a second it looked like Bo Dawson might get emotional and cry, but he hugged his son and they watched Ford take off down the path, Gram calling after him to be careful.

A fussy shriek came from the bassinet beside the coffee table, and Harrison had never been more grateful for a crying infant. He stood up, his collar tight, his stomach churning.

"Uh, Daisy, I just realized I told my aunt Lolly I'd visit earlier than usual, since I keep catching her asleep. Maybe we can put off the tour of the ranch until tonight or tomorrow." He needed some air. Some space. Some head space away from the Dawson clan. And their home movies.

She went over to the bassinet and lifted out

Tony, cradling him against her. "Of course. There's lots more video, but another time. The footage of what the ranch looked like before Noah started rebuilding to the day I helped put up the grand reopening banner—it's amazing."

He wasn't sure he wanted to see any of that. No, he knew he didn't. This was all too much. "Well, I'll be in touch about that tour."

That's it. Keep it nice and impersonal. *Be in touch* was a sure distance maker.

She eyed him and lifted her chin. "Oh—I almost forgot! I have a favor to ask, Harrison."

Gulp. How was he supposed to emotionally distance himself by doing her a favor?

She smiled that dazzling smile. The one that drew him like nothing else could. "If you're not busy around five o'clock or so, I'd love your help in putting together the rocking cradle my brother Rex ordered for Tony before he left town. It arrived yesterday, and I tried to put it together, but it has directions a mile long that I can't make heads or tails of. I can't ask Axel for help—don't tell him I said this—he's a wizard at GPS, maps and terrain, but give him instructions and he holds the paper upside down."

Ah. This was almost a relief. He'd put together the cradle *alone*. No chitchat. No old family movies. Just him, a set of instructions and five thousand various pieces of cradle. "I'm actually pretty handy. Sure, I can help you."

"Perfect," she said. "See you at fiveish."

A few minutes later, as he stood on the porch watching her walk back up the path, he had a feeling he was at a serious disadvantage in this deal.

Because the farther away she got, the more he wanted to chase after her and just keep talking. Which sent off serious warning bells. That Harrison might actually *more* than just like Daisy Dawson already—and it was just day one of the deal.

Chapter Six

Not only was Aunt Lolly awake when Harrison arrived at Gentle Winds, she was chatting with a woman around her age. Harrison had never met the visitor and didn't recognize her as one of the staff. She was petite and had short curly blond hair.

"Harry," Lolly said, sitting up a bit from her reclined position. He was glad to see her awake for once, but she looked sleepy and sounded kind of groggy. "Come meet my friend Eleanor. She has the cutest dog. I forget the breed. A cockasomething."

Lolly had a friend? As far as he knew, Lolly had kept to herself the last ten years. When he'd asked her if he could call anyone to let them know she was here, she'd said a firm no. That had been eleven days ago, and he'd asked a couple times since. The answer had never changed.

He extended his hand, and the woman shook it with a warm smile. "I'm Harrison McCord, Lolly's nephew. Very nice to meet you. Do you live in Prairie City, too?"

Eleanor nodded. "I live just two doors down from Lolly. We just knew each other in passing, but she always stopped to pet my dog and tell me how cute he is." She turned back to Lolly. "I had no idea you were even ill." She frowned, and Harrison knew she was thinking about how ill Lolly *was*. Terminally. She looked at Harrison. "As I was telling Lolly, I happened to ask our postal carrier if he knew if Lolly went away on a vacation or something, and he told me he'd heard she was in hospice. I was shocked."

As they both looked over at Lolly, it was clear she'd fallen asleep, as she often did, sometimes even midconversation.

"Lolly's pretty private," Harrison said. "But I'm so glad you asked after her and that you came. That's very thoughtful of you, and it clearly means a lot to Lolly."

"She's a lovely person. Do you know that she bought a box of dog treats just so she could carry some in her pocket and offer them to dogs she met on her walks?"

Harrison smiled. That definitely sounded like Lolly. "She always did love animals." He'd once offered to take her to the animal shelter to adopt a cat or dog, but she'd said she'd rather help by volunteering. He once asked if she was doing that, and she'd brushed him off. As he'd said: Lolly was private.

"The man she was dating must have been devastated," Eleanor said. "I saw them together a couple times, and they looked so happy, holding hands and swinging them."

Harrison gasped. "Wait. Lolly was dating someone?"

"Well, I only saw them twice, and that was right before I stopped seeing her around altogether. I once asked her about him, and she smiled and said she was testing the waters. She had the biggest grin on her face."

Huh. So what happened to the guy? No one had come to visit Lolly since she'd arrived at Gentle Winds eleven days ago. Except for him and now Eleanor. He'd double-check with the nurses.

"Do you happen to know his name?" he asked.

She shook her head. "I didn't recognize him from the neighborhood. He looked to be about her age, midsixties. More salt than pepper hair, thinning some. Tall. Wore silver-framed eyeglasses, I remember that."

He reached into his wallet and pulled out one of his business cards, then wrote down his cell phone on the back. "If you happen to see him again, will you tell him I'd like to talk to him about Lolly?"

"I will," she said, picking up her purse and standing. "I'll let her rest. It was nice to meet you, Harrison. I'm so sorry about Lolly's condition." She briefly put a hand on Harrison's arm.

"Before you go, Eleanor," he said, "do you know if the two of them were serious?"

"I really don't know anything. Just what Lolly said about 'testing the waters' and looking so happy."

So what happened? he wondered. Who was Lolly's mystery man, and why hadn't he been to see her?

He looked at his aunt, sleeping peacefully. He wanted to gently rouse her and ask about her new man. But Lolly hadn't mentioned him at all. Had they broken up? Had Lolly not told him how ill she was or that she was entering hospice? Lolly's cancer had been caught so late that she hadn't been treated; she looked frail, but she had her hair.

Maybe she hadn't told her new guy that she was sick at all?

His questions would have to wait until his next visit. It was nearing four o'clock, and he was due at Daisy's at five to put together the cradle.

Lolly "testing the waters" didn't change anything for him. Bo Dawson had bet the ranch and lost, and it belonged to the McCord family. End of story.

But he sure did hope that Lolly had let someone in her life. The thought of his aunt walking down the street, holding hands with someone who made her happy, lifted his spirits like nothing else.

The only thing that came close was the thought of seeing Daisy again, being close to her. He just had to avoid conversation and her television and he'd be fine.

"I don't know, Daize," Axel said as he poured himself a cup of coffee in the farmhouse kitchen. "Consorting with the enemy? What if you spend all this time with the rat bastard and he still takes us to court?"

Was the guy who'd listened so attentively, understood so much, and been so affected by the home movies and her stories that he'd run out of the house…a rat bastard? Daisy didn't think so.

She'd put her money on Harrison McCord having a bigger heart for the personal, for people, than the businessman let on. Or even realized himself.

Daisy sat down at the table with her iced tea. "I did consider that. I still think it'll be worth it. I'll know I tried. And I think my plan is having an effect already."

"I hope so," Axel said. "I saw McCord walking around this morning. I wanted to punch him right in the smug nose."

"I hear ya." She truly did. Though his face was so attractive, she would probably aim for the stomach or arm. Wham! Not that Daisy—or any of her brothers—were prone to hitting people. And besides, the whole subject reminded her of Harrison's father wanting to punch out their father, and Bo not wanting his handsome faced messed with. She rolled her eyes. Her father had been handsome, she'd give him that.

Axel looked so much like him. All the siblings did, but Axel was almost a carbon copy with his thick dark hair and the piercing blue eyes. Features that were somehow pretty and masculine at the same time.

"So how's it been being back here on the ranch?" she asked. Axel, like Zeke, Rex and Ford, had never wanted anything to do with the place.

He'd invested in the rebuilding like they all had, but he had memories of dealing with a drunk, negligent Bo, watching him quickly turn their grandparents' hard work and legacy into a dilapidated mess, and the cowboy had basically been knocked right out of him. She knew Axel loved his work as a search-and-rescue expert, Dude, his hardworking partner and buddy always by his side. That partner was curled up in the big dog bed Axel had brought with him, half a rawhide bone protectively under a front paw.

Axel took a sip of his coffee. "Like Ford said, the changes Noah made are so big that it doesn't remind me of the old place or what Dad did to it. It feels new. Dawson Family Guest Ranch 2.0 for real. It feels like true progress, you know?"

"I totally agree. I'm glad to hear it, too. It's nice having another brother here." *And you're going to stay forever!* she wanted to add. *We have this great big family and yet we're scattered, barely connected to one another's lives.* Daisy wanted to change that.

She bit her lip. If Harrison McCord did take the ranch away from them, her entire dream to have the six Dawsons settled here would go up in the ole smoke.

She'd just have to make sure Harrison didn't take the ranch.

Axel smiled and looked around at the country kitchen, with its antique charm despite the fact that everything in it was brand-new, from the cabinets to the tiny cabbage roses wallpaper to the tile floor. "I admit, I like the place. I know I spent a few years living in this house as a kid and teenager, but not much of it reminds me of that old dump. Oh, and by the way, Daisy—stop *not* asking me to babysit if you need some time to yourself or to do something."

"You noticed that?" she asked, sipping her iced tea.

"Yes. I want to spend time with my nephew. So ask, okay?"

"You'll regret that fast," she said with a grin. But wasn't this a great sign? Axel wanted to spend time with a baby! A newborn who cried and spit up and pooped. The man had it in him to settle down, start a family of his own. Of course, she had no idea if that was the case. But wanting to hang with little Tony meant something very good.

He laughed. "Maybe. But seriously. I'm fine. I'll stay for a couple of weeks and then go back to work." He turned away, picking up his coffee, his mind traveling, she could tell. He was thinking about what went wrong on the rescue mission. She was pretty sure, anyway.

She eyed him. "You gonna tell me what happened out there on the mountain? With the mother and little boy?"

He put down his mug. "Let's just say I got too personally invested in the mission, and I broke a couple rules involving my own safety to make sure that boy was reunited with his mother before the day was over."

"I get it," she said. That was Axel. He cared—hard. And he'd risk his job to save someone.

"Some people are sticklers for rules. Like my boss. Apparently there's a right time to bend a rule and a wrong time, and I went too far." He looked away, taking a long drink of his coffee. "Let's change the subject. How about I take my nephew for a walk around the ranch? He could use some Uncle Axel time, starting right now."

Daisy grinned. "He absolutely could. And perfect timing, because I asked the interloper over at five to put together the cradle that Rex sent. I showed him some old videos this morning of Gramps and Gram starting the ranch, and I'm going to share more of their amazing history."

"I doubt he'll care too much about old stories," Axel said, standing up. "The man wants to avenge his father getting swindled out of beating Dad to a pulp and winning a *working* guest ranch. Anyone would have felt that way after looking at the trash heap with storm-damaged buildings and overgrown fields and also noticing Dad had sold off all the animals and equipment to pay for his drinking and gambling habit."

Daisy bit her lip. She thought about how moved he'd seemed this morning by the videos and what she'd told him about her family. "I have a feeling about Harrison McCord. I might be wrong. But there's a good guy in that businessy exterior. And don't forget—he helped deliver that nephew you're taking out for a walk."

Axel sighed. "I suppose. I'll reserve a quarter of my judgment. How's that?"

Daisy laughed. "Sounds good."

In a few minutes, she had Tony's tote bag packed with the necessities, and she watched her brother wheel the stroller down the ramp and onto the path leading to the big barn. She'd assured him he could bring Tony right back if he needed to be changed, but Daisy figured Tony would be A-okay for a good hour.

She stood on the porch, breathing in the gorgeous summer air, so fresh and breezy today with temperatures hitting the high about now at eighty-four.

Maybe before it got dark she'd walk down to the creek and dip her feet in. She'd spent a lot of time at the creek as a kid, and now Tony would. The thought made her smile.

She felt so hopeful—about changing Harrison's mind, about Axel not wanting to leave the ranch or at least the town, that she realized she could hold another thought in her head other than the fear of losing the family business. She ran inside for a pad of paper and pen, then went back into the gorgeous afternoon breeze and sat on the porch swing.

At the top of the page she wrote, *Axel's Type*.

Axel was two years older, and she'd seen a bunch of his girlfriends during high school and the couple years after until he'd stopped coming around. So what was his type? What kind of woman did Axel go for?

Hmm. She tapped the pen against her chin. All Axel's dates and girlfriends had absolutely nothing in common as far as she could recall. There were blondes, redheads, brunettes. Short, tall, medium. Curvy, skinny. Super brainy and totally ditzy. Outdoorsy hiking enthusiasts and stiletto-wearing fashionistas. The woman she'd had in mind for him at the wedding was a pretty redhead who led wilderness excursion tours for the ranch. Daisy had figured on introducing them at the reception, and their first date would be a midnight hike afterward and they'd fall madly in lust and that would be that. But of course, there was no reception, and the two had likely not met.

Now she just had to figure out the best way to bring them together. Invite Hailey Appleton to dinner? Arrange a blind date? Nah, since Axel would likely say *no way.* Yup, she'd invite Hailey to dinner. In fact, she'd make it a little dinner party. She'd invite Enemy Hot Stuff, too, so that she could work on him. Two birds with one stone! She also thought about inviting Noah and Sara, but Noah would shoot daggers at Harrison all night, and who needed that tension?

Dinner at the house. Something casual, like an interesting pasta dish, or maybe she'd grill. And then true love would take its course.

She froze for just a second. *Holy cannoli: this means I actually still believe in that pie-in-the-sky fairy-tale stuff.*

Good. She wanted to believe. She hadn't lost that part of herself as a kid when her parents' marriage started going south. And she hadn't lost it when Jacob had ducked out on their wedding. Love was real, even if it had clunked her on the head and in the heart in the past.

Axel, you'll never know what hit you. She

grinned and was about to go in to check the time when she saw Harrison coming up the path. He wore faded, low-slung jeans and a navy T-shirt and a straw cowboy hat to ward off the bright sunshine. His shoulders were so broad. He was just so... sexy. She was surprised she could find anything sexy at three days postpartum. But as he walked, she couldn't take her eyes off his long, lean form. Or his tousled blond hair and how green his eyes were against the blue shirt.

He waved, and she did, too. She glanced down at her white cotton maternity capris and stretchy pink tank top. She couldn't be *less* sexy. But hey, this was the interloper and stealer of family businesses and legacies, not a man she'd ever think of romantically. And she had just given birth three days ago, so she could give a fig about looking good, let alone remotely sexy.

"Ready to work," Harrison said as he came up the porch steps. "Let me at that cradle."

She was surprised his enthusiasm could make her smile, but it did. "I have it in the living room. I think I'll keep it down there as another sleeping spot for Tony."

He followed her in. It was crazy to think that just yesterday, she'd kicked him out of this very room. Then she'd shared her couch with him and showed him scenes from her life, her history. Now he was putting together her baby's cradle. As if he were a cherished family friend. Ha.

She was *that* sure her plan would work. It had to.

"How was your visit with your aunt?" she asked.

He paused as if he wanted to say something but thought better of it. "She was actually awake for a bit, which was nice. And a friend was there when I arrived, someone who hadn't known she was terminal or in hospice until the postal carrier mentioned it. Lolly's pretty private."

"I'm glad to know she has a friend who cares," Daisy said.

Again, hesitation. "Me, too," he finally said. "This would be a nice spot for a cradle," he said, glancing at the big window on the wall adjacent to the stone fireplace.

"I think so, too," she said. If there was something on his mind regarding his aunt, he'd tell her—or not—when he was ready.

He smiled, took off his hat and sat down in front of the big box, the five pages of instructions on top of it along with her grandfather's old tool kit. "Tony sleeping upstairs?"

"Actually, my brother Axel took him for a stroll. I love that Axel is here. For the past several months, it's just been me and Noah. But now another Dawson uncle will get to spend time with his little nephew."

Harrison set down the instruction booklet and reached into the tool kit, taking out a few items, then he slid out the contents of the box, placing the pieces of wood and dowels and nuts and bolts in their little baggies around him. "I'm surprised only you and Noah came back to get the ranch renovated. Were the others just too busy?"

"Well, busy, but more like bad memories kept them away. My father was really hard to be around even in the years before he inherited the ranch from his parents. When he did take over about fifteen or sixteen years ago, the foreman and staff did the heavy lifting for as long as they could, but they weren't the boss—and the boss was either out living it up or passed out in a field somewhere. Within a year, the place fell apart operationally. Within five, it looked like it did before Noah rebuilt."

Harrison raised an eyebrow. "Your dad couldn't have been *that* bad if my aunt fell so hard for him."

"Oh, that was the one part of his life that always went right. He attracted the loveliest women. Kind, softhearted women who truly loved him and thought they could tame him, get him to settle down and stop drinking."

He stared at her, then turned his attention to

the directions. "So he didn't stop drinking? Was he an alcoholic?"

"Yes to being an alcoholic. No to stopping drinking or even trying. It's why he let the place go the way he did. He lost his days to sleeping off his benders, and when our foreman, Sara's dad, finally had enough and quit, my father eventually had to sell the animals that required the most care. He actually loved them—the horses and goats and sheep—which was really sad."

Daisy's eyes almost welled as she remembered how he'd sold Champ, his favorite gelding, who was twenty-six years old. Their closest neighbor, ten miles away, had bought him for their farm and he'd lived out a good life, but Bo Dawson had been so ashamed of having to sell him—for money and because he couldn't care for him—that he'd vowed to clean up his act. But that had lasted all of two days.

Daisy shook her head, trying to replace the sad memory with one that would make her angry instead. "He must have crashed his truck into the barn by the foreman's cabin three times coming up the road drunk," she continued. "Noah would tell me he hid our dad's keys or clipped a wire so he couldn't drive, but Bo would just call a lady friend and find the keys, and once he even hit Noah to get him off his back."

"That sounds really rough," Harrison said. "Noah was just a teenager. And back then it was just him on the ranch with his dad and the staff?"

Daisy nodded, guilt socking her in the stomach. "I was an hour away at college, living in the dorms, and Noah had an open invitation to visit, which I'm glad he took me up on often. We had a lot of weekends together, just talking about everything. The day he turned eighteen, he left the ranch. Once Noah was gone, there was no pull home for any of us." Tears stung her eyes, and she blinked them back hard.

"I'm so sorry," Harrison said, his expression so stricken she knew he really meant it. All that had been hard for her to actually say, hard to remember. Hard to live. But it was in the past.

"I think his alcoholism is why he never mentioned the bet and the napkin," she added. "He was probably drunk as usual, and since your dad didn't want the ranch upon seeing its condition and demanded something else, they both gave up when there *was* nothing else."

Harrison put down the instructions. "So you think I should give up, too. Now that the ranch is what your father made it out to be when he bet it."

"Yes," Daisy said. "I do. This is ten-year-old stuff, Harrison. Both parties are gone."

"My aunt is still here," he said.

She winced. "I didn't mean—"

He shook his head, his tousled blond hair falling in his face. "I'm sorry. This isn't your fault, Daisy. Or your brothers'. I'm sorry I'm making it your problem."

"I have a solution for that," she said overly brightly. *Please say you'll back off from this unfair situation. Please.*

But he just looked at her for a moment, then back at the instructions and contents of the box spread before him. "I doubt I'll ever put this cradle together if we keep talking. Maybe I should just get it done, work alone."

This was exactly what her deal was supposed to do. Get them talking about things that made them both uncomfortable. Get them talking, period. But she was done with this conversation and so, apparently, was he.

"I think I'll go put away some of the gifts I received for Tony in the nursery," she said. "If you need anything, just let me know. And help yourself to a drink or snack in the kitchen." Not that the thought of him walking around her house, poking around her fridge and cabinets didn't make her spitting mad.

She got up and headed toward the stairs. She wanted to flee from him and stay and talk at the same time. She'd been so confident that her plan would work. But suddenly she wasn't so sure that Harrison McCord would budge one inch, liking her and her family and the ranch or not.

You're not going to be able to convince him in one single day, she reminded herself. *You've got five days total. Use them. Make him see. Make him understand.*

But right now, she needed a break from him and everything he represented.

"C'mon, Dude," she whispered to the sweet yellow Lab. "Come keep me company in the nursery and then I'll take you for a walk along the creek. Maybe we'll run into Axel and Tony."

The dog tilted his head and followed her up the stairs like the good boy he was. If only Harrison would be so agreeable.

Chapter Seven

Harrison had just finished the cradle—took a solid forty-five minutes—when he heard the front door open and saw Axel push the stroller inside the foyer.

"Daize?" Axel said as he closed the front door. "We're back."

Harrison was kneeling on the floor, gathering cardboard and baggies and wrappings. "I think she's in the yard with the dog," he called out.

Silence. And then Axel appeared in the doorway of the living room. "Oh, it's you."

Harrison almost smiled. He had to admit, he liked that Axel wasn't trying to be his friend. None of that would work, anyway. "I put this together for Daisy. It's all set for the little guy."

Axel eyed him, then stared at the cradle. He walked over and examined it closely, pressing down on it, giving it a rock, checking the screws. "Seems solid."

"It is," Harrison said. "I didn't help deliver Tony so that he'd fall *out* of the cradle."

Axel raised an eyebrow. "Touché. But you're the enemy *now*."

Harrison stood up, his hands full of discarded wrapping to throw away. "Understood."

The word stung. *Enemy.* Had Harrison ever been anyone's enemy? He didn't think so. He'd always tried to be fair in business. He treated everyone with respect. But to the Dawsons, of course he was the enemy. He didn't like it.

A door opened, and Harrison could hear the tapping of nails on the tile kitchen floor. Dude came padding into the living room and beelined right for his person. Axel bent down and gave the dog a hearty rub and even a kiss on the head.

Daisy stood in the doorway looking both beautiful and surprised that he was still here. He supposed he *had* finished a good ten minutes earlier and had spent a little too much time picking up random bits of plastic that the nuts and bolts had been wrapped in. He hadn't wanted to leave before Daisy returned. Because it would seem rude to just finish up and go? Because he wanted to see her, talk to her? To look busy, he kept picking up little tubes of cardboard and stray foam pieces and stuffing them all into the big box.

She glanced at Harrison and gave a slight nod, then turned her attention to her brother. "Little guy give you any trouble?" She went over to the stroller and peered in. "Ooh, fast asleep. Good job, Uncle Axel."

Axel smiled. "He's as easy as you said. And I think every guest on the property stopped me to look in the stroller and ooh and ahh at the baby. A few even asked how fatherhood was treating me. Lord."

Daisy grinned. "One of these days, it'll get you. You'll see."

"Yeah. No," Axel said. "Anyway, I'd better get going. I promised Noah I'd sit with Sparkles until her tummy troubles go away."

"Ooh," Daisy said. "Poor Sparkles. She's one of my favorite goats. But don't sit *too* close, if you know what I mean."

Axel grimaced. "Gotcha. Apparently, Noah caught one of the guest kids feeding Sparkles jelly beans from his pocket. There are four new signs up about not feeding the petting zoo animals anything but pellets from the treat dispensers."

"Give her a belly rub for me," Daisy said. "And no worries about Dude for a few hours—we went for a long walk along the creek."

Axel gave Dude a scratch on the head and behind his ears. "Thanks, Daize. See you later. Bye, Tony," he added, then headed toward the door, finally giving Harrison a politeish nod of acknowledgment before leaving. When the door shut behind him, Harrison picked up the last of the wrapping and stuffed it into the box.

"All done," Harrison told her, giving the cradle a little push to make it rock.

"Very nice!" she said, surveying it. She pulled out her phone and snapped a photo. "I'll send it to my brother Rex, who bought the cradle." She looked at the photo she took, then put her phone back in her pocket. "I was hoping that while I was gone, I'd come up with the magic words to make you stop all this craziness about the ranch and just let us be."

Why did she have to be so straightforward? And earnest? And so lovely?

She had him all tied in knots. He took in a quick breath, forcing himself to focus on facts. "You didn't come up with them because a deal is a deal,"

Harrison said. "If my father had taken possession of the ranch ten years ago, you and your brothers would have accepted that, right?"

"What? Of course not!" she said, hands on hips.

He crossed his arms over his chest. "I thought the issue for you was that the ranch had been rebuilt and had reopened to great success."

She glared at him. "Harrison McCord, my grandparents bought this land. Anthony and Bess, who you got to know from the videos. They built the ranch. They opened a business, hospitality at its core. They raised my dad here, and he raised us here—well, until my brothers' mothers left him and moved on. This ranch is our family history, our legacy, our future. It's *us*." Tony let out a fussy sound, and Daisy went over to the stroller and picked him up.

She held her son against her, gently patting his back, cooing softly at him. For a moment he couldn't take his eyes off her, off *them*.

"Harrison," she continued, "my problem with what you're trying to do isn't about timing. It's about the ranch itself. A falling-down mess or this," she added, waving her hand around. "Didn't your father leave you a piece of your family history when he died? No matter how big or how small?"

"Everything in his condo," Harrison said. "But

my father wasn't very nostalgic. He had some old photo albums, some mementos of his parents. But except for the black leather recliner he loved watching TV in, the old Timex watch he wore every day despite being able to afford an expensive one, nothing really jumped out at me that meant all that much to him."

"Oh," she said, looking a bit defeated. "From the way you were talking, I got the sense that family meant a lot to you."

"The people, yes. Not necessarily the *things*."

"This ranch isn't a thing, Harrison. It's our *family*."

"I don't think the law would see it that way. It's property."

"You're absolutely maddening," she said. "Do you know that?"

He stepped closer, but she stepped back. "It's not—"

"I know, personal. It's supposedly not personal. Well, guess what, Harrison? It is."

He was out of things to say here. Part of him wanted to forget all about the ranch issue—for the moment—and tell her what Lolly's friend had said, about the man she'd been dating. He wanted to ask her opinion if maybe he should try to find the guy. But suddenly he didn't want to talk about his aunt's private business with a *Dawson*. Daisy was out to protect her family—period. He should do the same.

"And in fact," she added, "I'd like you to really understand how personal it is. So please come to dinner tonight. I'll expect you at seven."

Dinner? Here? With all this tension—of various kinds?

"Look, Daisy, I don't think—"

"You made a deal," she reminded him. "So I'll see you at seven. It'll be just you and me. Axel is working the dinner shift with Cowboy Joe since one of his assistant cooks called in sick. I'll be making honey-garlic chicken stir-fry with my secret recipe rice."

Home movies. Putting together a baby cradle. Now dinner—and a really good-sounding home-cooked meal.

"Are you sure you really want to make a fancy dinner?" he asked. "You did just have a baby three days ago. You should be napping every chance you get. Or putting your feet up. Or just taking it easy."

"Who said anything about fancy?" She grinned, and he relaxed a bit. "I've got this. Tony's an easy baby, and I have so much help and support from my family. So no worries."

He smiled. "Okay, then. I didn't know rice had secret recipes."

"This one does. And you'll see why when you taste it."

"I guess I'll see you at seven, then," he said.

He took the box and started to lug it toward the door.

"Axel will drive that out to the recycling center for me later," she said. "You can just leave it."

Her family really *was* there for her. Every step of the way, it seemed, with everything, big and small. She made it very clear that she knew she was lucky in that regard. The whole family was lucky. Maybe not when it came to old bets that were signed and dated. But with relatives.

Harrison dragged the box back to the corner and out of the way, then headed toward the front door, pausing in front of her. "See you later, Tony," he said, reaching out to give his head a gentle touch. He was almost surprised she didn't jump back.

"Thanks again for putting the cradle together," she said. "Tony says thank you, too." She turned sideways so that he could see the baby's face.

He peered at Tony of the big slate-blue eyes and giant cheeks. The little guy was wide-awake and alert and staring at him. "Anytime. Really. It was my pleasure."

That was the problem, though.

It really was his pleasure to assist her. To spend time with her.

He had to put up some kind of magical barrier so that he'd stop liking her so much. And being so damned attracted to her.

He had about an hour to work his potion.

After Harrison left, Daisy made sure she had everything she needed for her honey-garlic stir-fry and secret recipe rice. Good thing she checked, because she was completely out of garlic and had to borrow two bulbs from Sara, who loved to cook. Daisy could make a couple of decent meals—her stir-fry and a couple of pasta dishes—but overall she was a breakfast-for-dinner, pizza, Chinese or Mexican takeout, and cookout type. Before she found out she was pregnant, she'd even be happy with a bowl of Cap'n Crunch for dinner, but she'd stepped up the healthy living for the baby's sake. Now that she'd be cooking for her little family of two—although she had a ways to go before Tony would even start solids—she'd have to up her game. Might as well start by practicing on Harrison.

Although it did feel wrong to *want* to make him dinner. Cooking for someone, sharing a meal with them, felt intimate. Still, she needed him to owe her, right?

Ugh. All this suddenly did seem as manipulative as Harrison had complained about. But the stakes were high, and she was playing to win here. And winning meant that her family kept the ranch. If her honey-garlic stir-fry had an effect on him, good.

But if she were really honest, she'd have to admit that she liked being with Harrison. For a man who was looking to take away her family's business, a business that *would* one day be left to Tony and his cousins and cousins-to-be, she found him almost soothing to be around. Something in the way he listened. Really listened. He looked at her when she spoke, his emotions plain as day on his handsome face, and his responses were always honest and thoughtful. How he made her feel so comfortable was beyond her. Then there was the matter of wanting to kiss him.

That was craziest of all. Hormones, had to be. But there was no denying the man drew her like no one had in a long, long time.

Maybe she'd invited him to dinner so she could figure him out. Figure out her feelings for him. Because her feelings made no sense.

Once she had dinner prepped, she put Tony

in the sling and set out to enjoy a fifteen-minute walk around the ranch—for reinforcement more than anything. When Harrison would arrive later, she'd need to be fortified with how much this place meant to her. Every time she noticed his chest or the way his jeans skimmed over his lean hips, she'd picture the ranch and get herself back on track.

Tony had fallen asleep on the way to the barn. She waved at the Humphrey family, who were on horseback in the far pasture, getting lessons from Dylan, one of the ranch hands. Daisy stopped to smile at Hermione and Juanita, busy-bee goats who were jumping onto logs in their pen. She breathed in the gorgeous late-afternoon air, warm and breezy, the Wyoming wilderness never failing to restore her.

But wait—was that crying she heard? She glanced down at Tony's tiny head. The sounds certainly weren't coming from the sling. It was a *woman* crying. She stood still and listened. Yup. That was definitely someone crying. And it was coming from around the side of the barn.

Daisy walked to the edge and peered around. Uh-oh. Tessa Monello, the newlywed, was sitting against the barn, her head on her arms on her knees. Crying and sniffling. "Tessa?" Daisy said softly. She pulled out the little packet of tissues she always carried in her back pocket and handed it to Tessa, who took it and used a tissue to dab at her eyes.

"Did you and Thomas have an argument?" she asked, having no doubt they did.

Tessa's face crumpled, then her hazel eyes flashed and she looked like she might explode. "Do you want to know what he had the nerve to say to me?"

Oh boy. Did she? Daisy wasn't sure she should be getting in the middle of this.

Tessa didn't wait for an answer. "He said I was being Team Tessa instead of Team Monello. First of all, I've been a Monello for barely a week!"

Daisy lowered herself to the ground, her feet straight out.

Tessa looked over inside the sling. "Aw. So sweet." Then her face crumpled. "Thomas wants to have a baby right away. Is he kidding? I'm twenty-two!"

"Did you guys talk about all this stuff before you got married?" Daisy asked.

"We were too busy having sex," Tessa said, rolling her eyes. "I'm such an idiot!"

"Uh, exactly how long were you a couple before you got married?"

"Exactly a month. But it felt so right. I truly believed he was it, the one, the only guy for me. Now he's turned into Mr. Traditional? *What?*"

A month. She hadn't known Jacob much longer before she'd conceived. *Hindsight is definitely twenty-twenty, but we all need to be much more careful with ourselves and our futures*, she thought. She was so happy to have Tony, but she certainly didn't have even the faux fairy tale she'd been hoping for. She sighed inwardly. Fairy tales were never going to be real life. Her family, her brothers' families, could speak to that. Noah and Sara seemed to have it all right now, but they'd had one rough start. They'd fought for what they had. If you recognized that what you did have was that special, then you had to make it work.

She believed in love, but she also knew it didn't always come easy.

She supposed that would be her advice for Tessa.

"So he wants to start a family right away? Did he say why?"

Tessa grimaced. "He wants five kids, and he 'read some link on Twitter that younger mothers have healthier babies.'"

"And what do you want?" Daisy asked.

"Last month I sold two photographs to the *Converse County Gazette*," she said. "I want to be a photojournalist. I want to travel all across the state, taking photos, documenting what stands out."

"Congrats!" Daisy said. "That sounds amazing. And your new husband is not on board with this?"

"He's supportive of my being a photographer—for weddings, family portraits, pets. That kind of thing. But I have this idea for an entire series on female ranchers in Wyoming. I actually got inspired by your sister-in-law. You should see the shots I've taken of Sara. She told me that she's now assistant forewoman but that she'll be promoted to forewoman in the next few months as her husband, the current foreman, takes on more of an administrative role."

Daisy was thrilled for Sara. She knew how much being forewoman of the ranch meant to her, how hard she'd worked for it—and had worked for it since she was a teenager on not only this ranch back in the day but other prosperous operations. She and Noah had made a plan for childcare, and since the ranch was "bring your baby to work"–friendly, they could both see the twins often throughout the day.

"Guess who thinks *forewoman* is a made-up word?" Tessa asked. "I had no idea I married a Neanderthal!"

"Here's what I think," Daisy said. "I think you

and your brand-new husband need to focus on getting to know each other. You've got the love, right? You've made a lifetime commitment. With those vows in mind, put in the time to really listen to each other. The two of you simply have to talk, really talk, about what matters to you. Yes, Thomas might have some old-school ideas that need to be knocked out of him. You'll do that. And you might have to think about how traveling the state might affect your marriage—same if he was the traveler."

"Huh. I guess. I just got so mad I stalked off."

"The both of you will probably be doing a lot of that," Daisy said. "But if the love is there, Tessa, that's your base. Come at Thomas from love—which means respecting that he may have a different point of view. What I'm trying to say is, try to put aside the indignation and anger and *talk*. If you can't agree on fundamentals after that, that's a different story. But don't give up on each other before then."

Tessa's face lit up, and she threw her arms around Daisy as best she could with a baby between them. "You're absolutely right. One hundred percent right."

Phew. Daisy didn't want all her jealousy and envy over the Monellos to have been in vain. "Talk to your husband. And listen. And make sure he does the same. You both need to listen as much as you talk."

"Got it!" Tessa said, leaping up and dashing off.

Daisy smiled and slowly stood up, dusting off her tush. "Well, guess my work here is done," she said to Tony, giving his head a gentle caress. She thought about inviting the Monellos to her dinner party to help facilitate the discussion a bit, but that was going *way* too far—if they started bickering about such fundamental stuff, she'd scare Axel right out of the idea of settling down. She'd heard what he'd said about fatherhood—pertaining to himself—earlier today loud and clear. Fatherhood might not be on his radar right now, but he hadn't said anything about marriage being off the table. Baby steps. From dinner party to dating to settling down in Bear Ridge for all eternity.

She shook her head at herself, but hey, she had to think big.

She'd done what she could for the Monellos at the moment.

Now to get through to one stubborn businessman.

Chapter Eight

Can. Not. Lose. My. Edge. Harrison repeated his new mantra before heading down to the creek. He had twenty minutes before he was expected at Daisy's, and being alone in his cabin and staring out the window at trees was making him think too much about her. He had to keep the focus on *his* family, not hers. And he had to keep his mind off her face and her blue eyes and how attracted to her he was.

As he walked under the canopy of trees, he lifted his face to the sunlight poking through and breathed in the fresh air. Ahh. He could spend weeks here just walking along the creek and skimming stones and never be bored. He supposed soon enough, that would be an option that wouldn't cost him a cent.

He turned right instead of left to avoid where many of the guests tended to walk or fish or dip their toes. He wasn't in the mood for chitchat. The direction he walked in would lead near the gates to the ranch and there was a lot of brush cover, so not many people came down this way.

He stood on the bank and skimmed a few rocks, the ripples mesmerizing. Just what he needed to get Daisy Dawson and Tony Lincoln Dawson off his mind. The creek truly did set his head straight, calm him, soothe him. The whooshing sound of the current, the birds, the critters that called the creek bank home. He hadn't spent much time around brooks or rivers growing up; his parents had always liked living in the center of Prairie City with its shops and restaurants and businesses, including his dad's accounting practice, where he'd been in high demand for area ranches. A month or so after Harrison's mother died when he was twenty and in college, his dad had sold the house, unable to bear living there without her. Eric Mc-Cord had bought a condo and after a few years sold that for a smaller one when it wasn't so necessary for him to have space for a six-foot-two college student. So there was no family home to leave to him. That was gone, another family living in it.

What Daisy had been talking about—nostalgia, sentimentality for the past—Harrison wished he did have more of that. There were old photo albums in his attic, some family videos, but instead of them filling him up, the memories made him feel kind of alone. Sometimes Harrison thought he was too much a lone wolf. What had his mother said a few times? *Wolves are pack animals.*

But six months ago, after catching his ex-girlfriend in her lies, he'd felt himself harden up, his trust in anyone and anything obliterated. His father's story about Bo Dawson and how he'd been cheated by that rat had only made Harrison turn away from people more. He started delegating less at the office. Doing the big deals himself. Working out harder and harder at the health club, the punching bag his last and most satisfying stop before heading home. Alone. He hadn't exactly been having a great time lately.

He thought about how Daisy had to live in a world of trust, starting with having to put herself—and her baby—in his hands when he showed up on the side of the road. A half hour prior, she'd been left at the altar in her maternity wedding gown, her trust blown to bits. Maybe that was how trust worked—taken away and restored. Repeat. Repeat. Repeat. Except when it came to Harrison. It was as if *ye of little faith* had been written about him.

He sat down on a big rock and watched the water flow down the creek, his attention on a beaver— or at least he thought it was a beaver—scurrying among the brush and twigs at the creek's edge. He really was losing his edge here. Here at the Dawson Family Guest Ranch. Here with Daisy. He had to stop thinking about her. Her and that little infant with the big slate-blue eyes. Tony had had Harrison at first cry. He was being pulled in right before his eyes, right under his watch. He cared too damned much about the two of them.

He wanted to do right by his family, but he wanted to do right by Daisy, too. He wasn't sure how that was possible and no answers were coming to him, so he got up and headed up the path to the main house.

As he took the steps, he could smell something amazing wafting from the screen door. His stomach rumbled. He tapped on the door, and in seconds there she was in a light blue sundress, her long honey-brown hair loose around her shoulders. Did she have to be so pretty? "Must be the secret rice recipe that smells so good," he said because he was flustered. He could barely drag his eyes off her face.

"Oh, it is." She grinned and opened the door.

He felt like he should have brought a bouquet of flowers for her. She'd invited him to dinner, for heaven's sake. And he'd shown up empty-handed. But this wasn't a date—far from it. It was an ambush, and he knew it. Still. "I should have gone into town to the bakery I pass every time I drive to and from Prairie City and picked up some of their amazing bread."

"Nope. You're my guest, so all I need is you." Her eyes widened, and two pink splotches appeared on her cheeks. "That came out weird."

He laughed. "I've always liked weird."

"Me, too, actually."

He held her gaze a beat too long, and she didn't look away. Trouble. "So can I help with anything?"

"Sara stopped by earlier and beat you to it. Everything's ready." She led the way into the dining room. The table was set, interesting big blue flowers in a vase in the center. Daisy sat on one side and Harrison on the other. She lifted up the lids of the platters. The stir-fry made his mouth water, and the secret recipe rice looked savory and delicious. She heaped both on his plate, then served herself.

"Bon appetit," he said, forking a big bite. He

smiled. "My mother always said that. Guess I picked up the habit."

"Was she a great cook?" Daisy asked.

"My dad was actually the cook in the family. My mom hated to cook."

"Like me!" Daisy said. "Well, I don't totally hate it, but I'm not great in the kitchen."

"Then why is this food so good?" he asked, taking another big bite of stir-fry. He already wanted seconds.

"It's my one thing," she said. "So I'm really glad you like it. In fact, I'm going to make it again for a little dinner party I'd like to host, and I could really use your help."

Oh no. What subterfuge was this? The crazy part was, she knew he knew what she was doing. Reeling him in. Making him care. Making him feel needed.

Oh God, it really was working.

"Need a waiter?" he asked.

She smiled. "No. I have this grand plan. Another grand plan," she added with a wry chuckle. "Wow, I really am a busybody. But this is important."

"What's this second grand plan? The one that thankfully doesn't involve me?"

She ate a bite of her stir-fry. He could barely

take his eyes off her again as she looked at him, her blue eyes full of determination and hope. He wanted to reach out and touch her face, her soft skin.

He was losing it.

"I told you how my brothers have bad memories of the ranch and Bear Ridge, despite how much renovations changed the place. Just being here reminds them of times they want to forget permanently."

He nodded. "I can understand that."

"But you can probably also understand how much it means to me to have my family back together on the ranch my grandparents started fifty years ago. Right now, it's just me and Noah. And I get it—even I ran far away and wasn't the slightest bit interested in coming home. Until I was pregnant and needed family, needed that history and connection to not only Noah on the ranch but to the ranch itself. I finally understood what that meant. And now being here, living here, working here, fills me up, Harrison."

This wasn't about manipulation or subterfuge or reeling him in. She was speaking from the heart, deep down, and he knew it. She'd meant every word of that.

And every hour they spent together, he saw

more and more of how the place made her happy, did fill her up, gave her peace and security.

He mentally shook his head. Still. The napkin wasn't about Daisy Dawson and what she needed. It was about his family and turning a wrong around. It was about what he'd promised his father.

Lolly has a boyfriend.

The thought slammed into his head. So what if she did? How did that change anything? Ten years of living like a recluse, then she knew she was dying and she'd let herself have a few weeks, a couple months, maybe, of romance with a man she felt attracted to. That had nothing to do with Bo Dawson being a rat bastard who'd cheated Harrison's father out of a bet in good faith.

He wanted to get up and leave. And not. He needed this conversation—and his thoughts—back on track. "The other grand plan, then?" he asked.

"Love," she said. "Specifically involving my brother Axel and a nice, outdoorsy redhead named Hailey. I was planning to introduce them at my wedding, but we all know that didn't happen."

"And where do I fit in?" he asked.

"Well, I'd like to do a little matchmaking between Axel and Hailey. I want Axel to have a reason to stay in Bear Ridge, to build the fancy log cabin he's always talked about right on the property, at the far end, where he'd be comfortable. My plan is to invite Axel and Hailey to dinner at the house, a casual dinner party kind of thing. Because I don't want it to feel like a setup, I'm inviting you, since we're barely even friends let alone anything resembling a couple." She let out a dry chuckle as if she was speaking and thinking at the same time and wanted to take back what she'd said. "It's just a few people over for dinner. No big whoop."

No big whoop. Except that Axel wasn't going to be able to build on the property. It would soon legally be McCord land and belong to Harrison.

But he couldn't say that. Wouldn't say that. She had to know it, though. Right?

"I think we're friends," he said without meaning to, his voice unsteady. Even he knew it was a dumb thing to say given where his thoughts had just gone.

Everything about his life was upside down. He'd lost his dad. He was going to lose his aunt. And Daisy, whom he now realized he wanted with every fiber of his being, could never be his, would never be his.

"Nope," she said, disappointment on her face. "Not friends. Friends don't do what you're trying to do, Harrison."

He felt that zap hard in his chest. She was right

about that. One of them had to remember it, and he was glad she did, because he was too far gone. He stared down at his plate for a moment, pushing his stir-fry around to give him a minute to come up with a response. He had nothing.

There had been no mistaking that zap. Daisy was *in*. Her plan had worked—to a degree.

You can have feelings for the woman, be attracted to the woman, care about the woman—and still insist on making things right for your family, he reminded himself.

He cleared his throat. He drank some iced tea. He ate more special-recipe rice. Anything to avoid talking, because who knew what would come out of his mouth? Daisy Dawson had him all crazy.

He had to back off. Among Eric McCord's last words had been "do what's right for me and Lolly, son." Yeah, it was a bum deal for the Dawsons, but it had been a bum deal for Eric McCord for *ten years*. Same for Lolly.

They turned their attention to their plates, eating in a kind of glum silence. He had so much to say and couldn't say any of it.

"Just let me know when to show up for that matchmaking dinner party, and I'll be there," he said, standing up. "Thank you for dinner, but I need to get going."

Daisy bolted up. "Wait. You don't have to go, Harrison. You shoveled my one great dish in your mouth in two seconds and now you're running away. Because I got to you. Admit it!"

He stared at her. She didn't pull any punches. Said it like it was. "You got to me because we *are* friends. If I never see you again after the five days are up, I'll always remember you, Daisy. But you're trying to manipulate an end, and it's not fair. My father has been owed this ranch for ten years now. His dying words asked me to get it for him. I'm going to do that. If my dad had taken over the property back when your dad made the bet, we wouldn't even be having this conversation. Or dinner. Or anything. This would be McCord land."

She shook her head, and he could see frustration and tears forming in her eyes. "This isn't right," she said, but her voice was shaky. But the way she was looking at him—not with anger, not with *You're the enemy*, but with *Help me out here, dammit, because there's something between us*, he knew he had *her*. The playing field was suddenly even.

And it sucked. This was what he wanted? To best Daisy Dawson, a brand-new mother who'd been stood up at the altar days ago? Who'd gone into labor alone on the side of a flipping rural service road?

There *was* something between them. He felt it to his toes. He felt it everywhere. And he knew she did, too.

He put his hands on her shoulders, and she stared up at him in such surprise that all thought went out of his head. He leaned his head forward. She leaned her head forward.

And when their lips met, it was as if they were both so damned happy to be there that they went for it, both clearly eschewing thought and rationale and deepening the kiss. His arms went around her back, one up into her silky hair, the other around her neck, her shoulders, drawing her closer. Her hands were on the side of his face, in his hair, her breathing fast and slightly moany.

He kissed her and kissed her and kissed her and could stay here all night, just standing here doing this. She started backing him into the living room, right onto the couch, and suddenly she was on his lap, her arms around him, her soft lips on his neck.

"Whoa, whoa, whoa," she said, pulling back a bit and staring at him, her eyes wide but full of delicious desire. "This is *not* part of my plan. *What* are we doing?"

He missed her lips immediately. "What felt right in the moment. Crazy, but there it is."

She sat back, taking a deep breath. "Well, I sure shouldn't be doing this! In fact," she added, turning to him, "we *can't* be doing this—for two very good reasons."

Took him a second, but he did know what she meant. One: they were supposedly enemies. Two: it would be a good six weeks before she could even consider sex. Standard doctor's orders.

"I could kiss you all day," he said—because that was exactly what he was thinking, what was echoing in his head.

"I *really* don't want to say 'same here,' but same here. Ugh! How can that be? You *are* the enemy, Harrison. Now I'm making out with you?" She sighed and turned away.

"My aunt had a boyfriend," he blurted.

Daisy turned toward him again, curiosity lighting her beautiful blue eyes. "She did? I thought she was all alone the last ten years, that my father broke her heart to the point that she never dated again and was miserable."

"That's what my dad said. And they were very close, so I thought he'd know. But Lolly doesn't talk about her personal life with me. She's never mentioned a man in her life—or not. And no one has been to visit her until today—a neighbor who said Lolly was sweet to her and her dog when she passed them on dog walks. Apparently, this neighbor saw Lolly holding hands with a man around her age—twice. And looking happy."

Daisy smiled. "Really! That's wonderful. It's a huge relief to know she did find some happiness in the romance department. I felt so terrible about my dad taking that from her."

"I was relieved, too. But if Lolly was truly involved with this man to the point that they were holding hands, why hasn't he come to see her?"

"You said she's private. Maybe she didn't tell him she was sick? Or *how* sick?"

That sounded like Lolly. "I can't stop picturing her walking down the street with her new guy, holding hands, happy. Coming back from dinner or headed to the movies. I thought she was all alone. But turns out she wasn't."

"We have to find him, Harrison!" Daisy said.

He was so grateful that the despair was out of her eyes, but he didn't know about trying to track down the mystery man.

"But if she didn't tell him she was going into hospice, she clearly didn't want him to know," he pointed out. "Maybe she said her goodbyes in her own way, you know?"

Daisy bit her lip, her expression turning wistful. "Sometimes people think they're saving someone from a heap of trouble and so they don't share their biggest problem or darkest hour. Maybe your aunt didn't want her terminal illness to enter into their happiness. Or maybe she felt they hadn't known each other long enough."

He'd thought about all that at the riverbank earlier. He should have asked the neighbor how long ago she'd seen Lolly with the man. It had to have been before his dad died, since Lolly had taken such a turn for the worse after the funeral and had moved in to Gentle Winds four days later. Harrison had been the only person by Lolly's side at the funeral and later at his dad's house, where they'd welcomed mourners.

When Eric McCord died suddenly from heart trouble, Lolly had been dealing with stage-four cancer for only a few weeks at that point and was not seeking treatment. Perhaps between losing her brother and being so ill herself, she'd turned away from the new love in her life. Harrison had a feeling that was exactly what had happened. But this was all just speculation. Harrison had no idea what had gone on.

He shook his head. "You know what I can't stop thinking about? This new man, being there for her, if only she'd let him. I could just picture him sitting at her bedside, reading from her favorite books or just holding her hand. Bringing her those fuzzy socks she likes. What if he'd want to be there for her? And what if that would actually make her happy?"

"I guess it depends on how she felt about him. But from what you described, it sure sounds like she was in love."

"I can't imagine Lolly holding hands otherwise," he said.

"You'll have to ask her. Go see her now. Maybe she'll be awake."

He glanced down at the floor, then back up at Daisy. It felt strange, poking into his aunt's private life this way. "Or…maybe I should leave it alone. Let her have the happy memories without her illness a part of it. I'll ask her about it, of course. But she's sedated for her comfort and not fully herself." He shook his head. "I don't know. I don't know what's right here."

Daisy put her soft hand on his arm, and he wanted to hold her against him so badly that he had to close his eyes for a moment to squelch the urge. "Maybe you can mention him, that you'd heard she'd been seeing someone, and watch how she reacts. Then go from there. You'll know whether to leave it alone or try to find him."

He nodded, feeling better about the whole thing. "That's exactly what I'll do. I'll go see her tomorrow morning." He stood up again. He wanted to stay. He wanted to go. He mostly wanted to just wrap Daisy in his arms and stay that way all night. But this was getting all out of hand. "But she's often napping. I might just investigate who the guy is on my own and get a sense of whether I should try to find him or not." He headed over to the door, hating to leave her presence.

She followed him to the door. "That's a good idea if you can't ask her about him directly." She tilted her head. "Did you really have enough to eat? You barely had one serving."

I only want you, Daisy, he thought out of nowhere. Which meant he really *should* go.

"Yes," he said, and it was true. "You're a much better cook than you think you are. The stir-fry and rice were delicious."

She smiled and took both his hands. "Thank you." She let go and stepped back, and he supposed that was her version of a hug. There would be no more kissing.

She put her hand on the doorknob, then hesitated. "Let me ask you something, Harrison. Let's say that stupid napkin does hold up in court and you *are* entitled to the ranch. What would you do with it?"

He hadn't even thought about that. "I suppose I'd change the name to the McCord Family Guest Ranch and keep on all the employees. Nothing would change except ownership. Management wouldn't even have to change. I'd be happy to keep Noah on to run the place and Sara as assistant forewoman."

He was getting to know her so well that there was no mistaking the sparks flashing out of her eyes. Barely contained anger.

"Turns out Noah promoted her to foreman— fore*woman*," Daisy said through gritted teeth. "He's going to be more administrative and focus on growth and new programs and initiatives."

"Perfect," he said.

She glared at him. "So that's just hunky-dory to you. All their hard work, all their plans, all their dreams. And you'll just take it away but let them keep their jobs. Aren't you a saint! Give me a flipping break."

Dammit. "I've been honest with you from the start. I intend to take the ranch, as it belongs to my family. No one loses their job, at least."

"Oh, how big of you!" She narrowed her eyes

at him, but now the anger was mixed with frustration and worry.

He hated this. Hated making her feel so awful. This was definitely not what he wanted. "We can't separate like this," he said. "With you angry and upset. Take me on the tour of the ranch. We can talk more."

"About what, exactly? How you'll order a big wrought iron *M* for the gates to replace the *D*? What is there to say, Harrison *McCord*?"

A lot. But what? Right now he didn't know how to smooth things over. They were at an impasse. They always had been.

"My plan is supposed to work!" she yelped.

He smiled. "It is, Daisy. Trust me."

She shoved her long hair behind her shoulders. "No, because if it were working, you wouldn't have just said you still intended to take over the ranch."

"I kissed you. I held you in my arms. Your plan is working."

"That's just straight-up lust," she said with an eye roll. "Please."

He looked directly at her. "No, Daisy. It isn't. I mean, yes, I want you. Clearly. But it's not just about lust."

He could see her trying to surreptitiously study him, read him, tell if he was being honest.

"Fine. Then the plan continues," she said, lifting her chin, her voice a bit uncertain, if he wasn't mistaken.

"Ah, yes," he said, grateful she wasn't kicking him out of her life. "The tour you promised me of the ranch. Tomorrow morning?"

"Tomorrow afternoon. Tomorrow morning I'd like to help you track down Lolly's mystery beau. Sara has the day off and can watch Tony for a few hours. We'll go to Gentle Winds in the morning—with me waiting in the waiting room, of course. If your aunt isn't able to talk, I think we should investigate the guy on our own—ask around Lolly's neighborhood. Maybe we'll run into the neighbor."

He didn't realize how much he wanted her—needed her—by his side for this unexpected detour until she'd proposed the idea of joining him. This was all uncharted territory for him, and he really didn't want to face it alone. "I'd appreciate your help in tracking him down. Lolly might not be able to give us answers."

She gave him a warm smile and squeezed his hand.

She likely thought that finding the boyfriend and hearing how in love his aunt was or had been would mitigate the past and her father's role. But it wasn't just about Lolly and how Bo Dawson had treated her. Bo had cheated Harrison's father. Lied, swindled and made a phony bet when the ranch was a hunk of junk. Besides, Harrison wouldn't ignore his father's wishes. Eric McCord had wanted unfinished business taken care of. Harrison's dad had made that clear.

When did you get this hardened? he wondered. *Bethany's betrayal? Bo Dawson's con job on two of your relatives? Your last two relatives on earth?*

Now there was only one. And soon he'd be the last McCord.

He needed to keep that steel surrounding him, but walking out the door of Daisy's home was among the harder things he'd done lately.

him in court," Daisy added. She wrapped her hands around her mug. Most of her wanted to go with Harrison today. But a piece of her knew she was asking for trouble. What if she let herself really acknowledge how she felt about Harrison? What if she started seeing his point of view about the ranch ownership? What if she found herself trying to talk her brothers into accepting that Dawson Family Guest Ranch truly belonged to the McCords?

She'd tossed and turned last night, grateful to get up with a hungry Tony at 2:30 a.m. She'd sat with him in the glider for a long time after he'd fallen back asleep, wondering how today would go. Wondering what was going to happen in the end. She and her brothers would never, ever give up the ranch—not without one hell of a fight. No matter how Daisy felt about Harrison, the ranch was the Dawsons' property. It *was* the Dawsons. She'd felt better after that, more secure about not warming to Harrison's way of seeing things.

Sara sipped her coffee, the same chocolate-pecan decaf brew Daisy was having. "Yeah, this plan of yours seems to have backfired." Sara shot Daisy a smile. "But at least you're in love."

Daisy's mouth dropped open. She wouldn't go *that* far. Right? "I am not! I just kind of can't stop thinking about him. And his face. Every time I want to hate him, I keep seeing him handing Tony to me, bundled in his blue dress shirt, on the service road. I see the glistening in his eyes, the wonder of what he'd just helped do. I keep seeing *that* Harrison. Why does he have to be so easy to talk to? Everything I say, he *gets*. And every time he gets me, I think about Jacob, who I almost actually married. He never understood anything I said. He'd look at me funny, and I just knew he couldn't make heads or tails out of what I meant about so many things."

Oh God. She really was in love. And she'd just detailed why.

"Uh-oh," Sara said, nodding. "This is dangerous territory."

"I know. Here I was, trying to hit Harrison with the warm fuzzies about me and the family and the ranch. Who got smothered by the warm fuzzies instead? Me. Did I not just get dumped on my wedding day? Is the man who wants to take away our family business the very man I'm head over heels for? What. Is. Wrong. With. Meeeeee?" She dropped her head gently on the table with a little thud and then straightened with a sigh.

"If you're in love, Daisy, Harrison must be wonderful. I know you. I've known you almost all your life. He has to be something special if he's won your heart."

"Aw," Daisy said, squeezing Sara's hand. "What would I do without you to make me feel better about the crazy things I get myself into?"

Sara took a sip of her coffee and smiled. "Hey, I know the feeling. When Noah and I reunited, I should have been super wary of him based on our past. But the minute I was with him on this ranch, it was like I was home. *He* was home."

But Harrison was trying to take *home* away. Daisy didn't know what to do with that truth, that undeniable fact—one Harrison himself kept pointing out at every opportunity. He wasn't hiding it at all. *I will take the ranch. I will see you in court.*

"And thank heavens," Daisy said, shaking off her thoughts about Harrison. "Because I got my BFF back and now you're my sister-in-law."

Sara smiled, and they both looked over at the three bassinets when a fussy cry came from one of the little ones by the window. Annabel and Chance, Sara's twins, were happily gazing straight ahead and Tony was the fusspot, his little face getting red in the cheeks.

Daisy stood and picked up Tony, holding him vertically against her and giving his back little pats. She'd learned his gas face, and yup, a satisfying burp came out. She sat down, loving the soft weight of him in her arms.

"I'm glad to watch my adorable nephew this morning," Sara said.

"I appreciate it. That way I can really focus my attention on Harrison and helping to track down this mystery boyfriend."

Sara finished her coffee and glanced at the clock. It was almost eight. "I hope you find him. I'll be rooting for you two. In both regards. You're both knee-deep in each other's family affairs now."

His family affairs. She'd really have to watch herself. She'd been trying to pull him into her family's history and who they all were so that he'd care about them. Now she would be pulled right into his—and she already cared about Harrison McCord. She just had to remember what was at stake here—her family's livelihood and future.

She looked down at Tony. The ranch was his future. "Maybe I shouldn't go on the search. I'm already too involved, Sara. Now I'll be even more involved." Had it just been days ago that she'd thought being left at the altar and figuring out single motherhood was her biggest problem?

"Look, from what you've said, Harrison is the good guy with a heart and a soul. Your big plan was always a good one, and now you've kind of gotten entwined in his version of the plan—not that I think he has one. I kind of feel like everything that's happening between you two is supposed to be happening, like you're meant to figure this out together. Not as adversaries."

"We can't be friends, though."

Sara gave a wicked smile. "All that hot kissing you told me about means something, Daisy. You're *beyond* friends."

This was insanely confusing. "So I should go with him to Prairie City. And be sucked into his life." She let out a breath. "I do want to help him find his aunt's boyfriend. And not because I want the news of this beau to feel more real for Harrison to make him stop being so angry at my dad. I just want Harrison to have that peace. To know that his aunt's final weeks were filled with love and romance and swinging hands and dates."

"You know why?" Sara asked. "Because you *really* are in love."

Oh Lordy, she already knew that. But now she *really* knew that.

Harrison liked Prairie City, which was still a small town but a bigger small town than most in the area with a bustling two-mile downtown. But the minute he turned onto Main Street, both sides lined with shops and restaurants and businesses, he missed the open wilderness of Bear Ridge and the Dawson ranch.

"Ooh, I love the burritos at that place," Daisy

said, pointing at Burrito Mama. "And not because of the mama solidarity." He glanced at her when she got quiet. "Now I miss Tony."

He smiled. "We'll just take a couple hours tops. Then I'll bring you back home to your little guy."

"Feels weird not to be with him," she said. "Like something is missing."

He stopped for a woman in the crosswalk, a black pug on a bright yellow leash on either side of her. "Like having your heart walk around outside your body. I've heard people say that about parenthood."

She gasped. "That's exactly what it feels like!"

He had no idea, but he could certainly imagine it. She was a devoted mother, and he admired her for it. He admired a lot about her. "Is motherhood like you expected?" he found himself asking. The question hadn't even been in his mind thirty seconds ago, but he wanted to know everything about Daisy. How she felt and what she liked and didn't. What she thought about this and that.

"It's so much more," she said, joy radiating on her beautiful face. "Instant love and so powerful it blows me away a hundred times a day."

"I'll bet," he said. "For a tiny human, Tony sure is something."

Her smile lit up her face. "Right?" She laughed,

and he wanted to kiss her so badly that he had to look away.

"Planning to become a dad one day?" she asked.

He coughed—so unexpected was that question. "Not sure. Sometimes I wonder if I'll ever settle down at all."

"I see it," she said.

"Do you?" He glanced at her before turning his attention back to the road.

"Yup. I believe in you, Harrison McCord."

She did. He felt it in his bones, in his cells.

But if she believed in him, then she also believed he wouldn't take possession of Dawson Family Guest Ranch. So he didn't know what more to say about that. He'd gotten to know Daisy well enough to know she wasn't playing him or saying what she thought he wanted to hear or trying to butter him up with compliments. She was a straight shooter. Earnest.

She believed in him. Why did that mean so damned much to him?

"You were a natural out there on Route 26 when a certain pregnant woman in labor needed help," she said. "So I think you'll make a great dad one day."

He laughed. "A natural? If the 911 operator hadn't told me what to do, I'd have been in a blind panic. I forgot half of what she said, too."

"Well, you did everything right. Doc said so."

"So how's it been?" he found himself asking. "Being a single mother?"

"Honestly? It's hard. Emotionally. Financially. There's no dad to help with anything—but the hardest part of that? No dad to care with me, worry with me, marvel with me. I think I wanted that most of all. Someone who'd feel about Tony the way I feel about him because that person is also his parent."

He hated to think of her struggling in any way. "Well, you're a great mother, Daisy." And that seemed to be very true. Devoted, loving, committed. Tony Dawson had the best of the best.

"Thanks for saying that. I do have great support. I know I'm lucky in that regard."

He smiled. "I was just thinking how lucky Tony is to have you for a mom."

A smile lit up her face again, and he could tell by her expression and body language that she was truly touched by the compliment.

"Your family really seems to stand by each other," he said quickly to douse the intimacy of the moment. "The way your brothers and Sara decked out the nursery. The way Axel helps out Noah on the ranch—at the crack of dawn, too. The way Sara has taken over your duties as guest relations manager in addition to her own work."

"That's family. Always there. And the ones who are not—physically, I mean? I've got plans for them, too." She grinned and rubbed her hands together.

"Ah yes, the matchmaking. When are you having the dinner party for Axel and the woman you think may lure him into staying in Bear Ridge forever?"

Her eyes lit up. "I'm thinking in a few days. I'll ask them both when we get back."

"Well, I'll be there."

"Thanks," she said. "You've certainly been there for me lately, too. Starting with the side of the road."

"You can always count on me, Daisy."

"Don't say something like that when it's not true. You're going to try to take the ranch away from me and my family. I can't count on you."

He frowned and turned his attention back to the road, pulling into a parking space in front of the yoga studio next to his favorite coffee shop. He'd planned to head straight for Gentle Winds, but the coffee in their cafeteria was seriously weak, and he needed the goods right now. "Coffee?" he asked. "I could use an Americano."

She glanced at the logo for Java Jamboree. He could see the wheels turning in her mind, fighting with herself not to tell him off, that they were on a special mission here and to let it go for now. She wanted to scream bloody murder at him, though; he could tell. "Definitely," she said, the subject changed for now. "Decaf iced latte with a mocha swirl for me. Oh, and whipped cream."

Relief hit him that he hadn't started a miniwar after all. "Let's get fortified, then we'll go to Gentle Winds. It's just about a mile from here."

They were in and out of Java Jamboree with their coffees, Daisy sipping her iced latte and lifting her face toward the sun. It was another gorgeous summer morning. Low seventies and bright sunshine.

"I love that fish and chips shop," she said, upping her chin across the street. "Ever been there? They serve everything in a little cardboard boat with newspaper lining. Amazing tartar sauce, too. I used to dream of the tartar sauce when I started my final trimester, and I'd wake up planning to be here the moment the place opened."

"It was my dad's favorite place to go for lunch," he said, staring at the few tables just outside the small restaurant. "It was one of the last places we—" He felt himself getting choked up and couldn't continue speaking. He looked away, his heart throbbing. He missed his father so much.

"I'm so sorry, Harrison," Daisy said, reaching up a hand to his cheek. "I know how badly it hurts."

He squeezed the hand that had been on his face, never wanting to let it go. "I know you do. Times two just like me."

She nodded. "Worst club to be in."

That got a small smile out of him, and he felt the knot of grief loosening a bit. "That's for damned sure."

"Well, should we get going to Gentle Winds?"

He nodded, and they got back in his SUV, driving the mile to the hospice, which was down a side street. The building was warm and welcoming, painted a dusty salmon, and the brick path to the front door was lined with rows of flowers. Lolly's room was on the second floor. They took the elevator, staff and fellow volunteers greeting him as he and Daisy headed down the hall. One nurse stopped him to ask if he was switching up his volunteer shift, noting that he usually came later in the day, and he explained he was just trying to catch his aunt awake. The woman wasn't on Lolly's care team, so she wouldn't know if his aunt was napping or not.

"I didn't know you volunteered here," Daisy said as they continued down the hall.

"Yup. I come every day. Before or after I see my

aunt, I sit with a few patients, read to them, play poker, listen to them share life stories."

"That's really lovely, Harrison."

He stopped in front of room 216. "This is Lolly's room."

"I see the sign for the waiting area up ahead. I'll go there and finish my latte. Take your time if she's awake."

He thought about just having her come in and meeting his aunt, but the last name would throw Lolly off and could upset her; he certainly wouldn't risk that. He'd talk to her about the boyfriend, and then maybe she'd open up some about her past and the situation with Bo Dawson.

"Thanks, Daisy. I'm glad you're here."

She smiled and walked down the hall, disappearing to the right where the waiting room was.

He knocked on the door. No answer. He gently opened it and found Lolly asleep. Her ash-blond hair was in a little ponytail, and her nails were red. Lolly liked her manicures, and the staff often came around for spa treatments. He'd come back this afternoon. There was no real routine to when Lolly was awake. The first two days, she'd been awake and alert in the late afternoons, so he'd continued coming at that time, but then she'd been asleep the next two times. He started coming in the morning before work and found her awake but not consistently. So he tended to just come in at random times and hope for the best.

He stepped back out of the room and gently closed the door behind him, then walked down to the waiting area. "Asleep."

"Let's take a walk in her neighborhood, then," Daisy said, standing up and putting her almost empty cup in the trash can in the corner. "We can knock on the neighbor's door—the one with the dog. And maybe we'll run into the postal worker. We can even go to the post office to talk to him if he's not out delivering."

"I think we should start in her condo," he said. "She's always been a bit old-school and wrote appointments on a magnetic wall calendar on her fridge. Maybe she jotted down the guy's name and the time they were meeting for dates. Or maybe we'll find something with his name and address or phone number on it."

"Does she have a cell phone?" Daisy asked. "You could go through the contacts and see who sounds likely as a friend versus a plumber kind of thing."

"Good idea. She did have one but didn't want to take it to Gentle Winds. It's in her condo."

"Let's go," she said, excitement on her face. "We're so close to finding the mystery beau!"

He wanted to take her hand. That was how

close, how connected to her he felt at the moment. But she started heading to the elevator, and he kept his hands to himself.

Lolly's condo was on the ground floor of a garden apartment–style complex with lush lawns and beautiful garden beds. There were two red doors side by side—identical one-bedroom apartments— Lolly's was on the right. He used his key that his aunt had given him when she'd moved into Gentle Winds. She'd given him permission to go in whenever he might need for whatever reason. He hoped she'd be okay with *this* reason. Was he invading her privacy or about to bring a smile to her face in the last remaining days she had? He'd bet everything he had it was the latter. Yes, Lolly was private and didn't talk much about herself, but Harrison knew his aunt, and he believed she'd be happy to see the gentleman, even if she hadn't set it up so that he could visit her. He had to trust his gut on this.

"Wow, so tidy," Daisy said as they entered a sunlit foyer.

That was Lolly. Spick-and-span. The living room had the usual furnishings and some interesting abstract paintings he'd always liked. He took Daisy on a brief tour of the small place—spotless kitchen, spotless bathroom, spotless bedroom with its blue-and-white quilt and seashells decorating the bureau.

Back in the kitchen, they stood in front of the refrigerator, studying Lolly's magnetic calendar featuring photos of dogs. It was mid-July, and Lolly had been at Gentle Winds for most of the month. Except for a note on July 2 to buy brie and apples, there was nothing else jotted down. He flipped up the page prior, for June, and that was much busier, though he knew Lolly had slowed down a lot last month. His name was all over the calendar, as he'd come over for dinner three times a week. He'd hired a housekeeper to prepare meals and keep the place to Lolly's standards, and a private nurse, who Lolly had adored, had come every day. There were notations about checkups and diagnostic tests, which he'd taken her to. But no male name was anywhere on the calendar at all.

"Maybe she has a planner," Daisy said. "The old-school kind you keep in a purse." She glanced around the kitchen. "There!"

Harrison looked at where she was pointing. A small red leather case sat on a stack of opened mail. He picked it up and unsnapped it. "Bingo." Daisy came over and stood tantalizingly close to peer at the pages. He could smell her shampoo.

He flipped back to June.

Robert, coffee at Java Jamboree. Robert, dinner. Robert, gallery hopping. Robert, movies—talk him into the rom-com and not the thriller. Robert, dinner and theater. Robert, dinner. Robert, walking tour.

The entrance of Robert into her life seemed to start in early June. The first entry was coffee.

"We found our mystery man!" Daisy said, her blue eyes shining.

"Robert." Harrison flipped to the start of the planner, which had an address/phone section. He went through page by page until he found Robert Chang—with not only home and cell numbers but an address. Yes! He was the only Robert there, so it had to be him.

He added the contact info into his phone. "Now what, though? Do I really call him without talking to Lolly first?"

Daisy bit her lip. "Harrison, I lost both my parents. Both to car accidents, almost twenty years apart. With my mom, there was no time for goodbyes. With my dad, the six of us just made it to the hospital from where we were scattered across the state. Axel had been up a mountain, and a chopper flew him over and he got there five minutes before our dad passed away. One of the last things my father said was, *You're all here.* And he said it while sobbing with such surprise on his face. He left this world knowing that no matter what, we cared, we were there for him. That means so much to me."

He was already so close to her that he put his arms around her before he could tell himself not to. She relaxed against him for just a moment.

"I'm okay," she said, but he could see she was feeling emotional. "I'm really going to need those fish and chips after this."

He smiled. "We'll definitely go before we leave Prairie City." The fish and chips shop would remind him of his dad, of his whole reason for going to Bear Ridge and booking Cabin No. 1, and suddenly that was both good and bad. He liked the good memories called up by being in places he and his dad had frequented. But now the reinforcement of his dad's final words, to get back what was rightfully his, was beginning to feel like a fifty-brick load on his chest.

She stepped back, and he missed having her in his arms immediately. "Well, here's what I think. We don't know why Lolly didn't tell Robert Chang she was sick or let him know she was at the hospice. Hey, for all we know, she *did* tell him, and he dumped her. Maybe he's a total jerk. We don't know anything. So let's find out. Lolly often isn't able to talk, so let's just ask him."

"I'll call and explain who I am and ask if we

could meet to talk about Lolly. I'll see how it goes from there."

"Perfect," she said.

As they left Lolly's condo, the woman who must live in the apartment right next door was on her knees in front of a patch of soil, pretty yellow flowers in little green containers at her side. Lolly had mentioned she had new neighbors a couple months ago, but Harrison hadn't met the middle-aged couple or their teenage twins.

"That's not the neighbor who visited Lolly," he whispered.

The woman turned at the noise and stood up, dusting off her hands. "Are you Lolly's family?"

"I'm her nephew, Harrison, and this is my friend Daisy." He knew Daisy didn't consider them friends, but they *were* whether she liked it or not.

"After a week of not seeing Lolly, I figured she was on vacation, and then when I saw our mail-woman, I asked her if Lolly was away, and she told me the bad news. I'm so sorry."

"Thank you," Harrison said. "Sounds like she barely told anyone she was sick, let alone that she was going into hospice."

"My own aunt was like that. Didn't want a soul to know or worry."

Harrison glanced at Daisy, then back at the

neighbor. "Did you happen to see her with a man in June? She was dating someone."

"Oh yes, I saw them a few times holding hands—the last time about two weeks ago. A couple times when we ran into each other here, she'd mention she was just getting home from gallery hopping or dinner or the movies with her significant other. She always had such a gleam in her eye when she said that." The woman smiled.

Huh. Lolly and Robert had been holding hands as late as two weeks ago, Lolly referring to him as her significant other. Something told him she'd broken up with him when they'd gotten the news Eric had died, followed quickly by Lolly taking a turn for the worse and knowing she'd have to go into hospice. Why she'd denied herself the comfort of having him at her bedside was for Lolly to say. But Harrison definitely wanted to talk to Robert.

"It was nice to meet you," Harrison said. "Thank you for the information."

The woman smiled and resumed her gardening. Harrison and Daisy got back into the SUV, and he told her his theory—that Lolly had turned away from everyone, perhaps not to worry them or to need anyone. The doctors and nurses hadn't been able to explain why she slept quite so much, and now Harrison knew why. Because she was sad.

Plain and simple. She'd closed herself off to avoid causing others heartache.

Oh, Lolly.

Daisy had tears in her eyes. "I think you're right about that. It's almost as if she broke her own heart to save his."

"I'm going to call him right now." He pulled out his phone, hoping he was doing the right thing by Lolly *and* this total stranger. He truly believed he was.

Harrison tapped in the numbers and waited. But the phone rang and rang, and voice mail picked up. "Hello, you've reached Robert Chang. I'm away for the next ten days, back on the twenty-second, and will return your call then."

The twenty-second was the day after tomorrow. *Please let us have that long,* he sent heavenward, then left a detailed voice mail for Robert.

He put his phone away and explained to Daisy about the voice mail messages. And the necessary wait.

"At least he didn't just leave today. We just have to wait two days. Let's go get fish and chips. You can help me plan the dinner party to find true love for Axel. I've never felt more like matchmaking than right now."

He knew what she meant. The story of Lolly

and Robert seemed a really beautiful thing. Love was in the very air.

Even he felt it. He stared at Daisy for a moment, taking in her long, honey-blond hair and blue eyes, the beauty mark on the side of her left eye. He had to fall out of love with her immediately.

Then he remembered they were going to Franny's Fish and Chips, his dad's favorite restaurant in Prairie City. Everything about Franny's reminded him of his father. And when he thought about his father, he thought about his final wishes. The bet. Taking the Dawson ranch. Bo Dawson's crappy treatment of Lolly.

Spending thirty minutes in that small restaurant would do a lot toward reminding him what his real purpose was. And it wasn't to fall in love with Bo Dawson's daughter.

Chapter Ten

As Daisy looked over the menu in Franny's Fish and Chips, she thought she should probably be past intense pregnancy cravings, but she wasn't. Ever since she'd spotted the restaurant earlier, she'd been imagining the fried catfish sandwich and Franny's amazing, creamy coleslaw she'd soon be enjoying. She ordered exactly that. Harrison went for the fried haddock and french fries, and hopefully he wouldn't mind when she swiped a few.

"What's Lolly like?" she asked when the waiter took their menus and left. "I know you said she was private, but what else? I'm trying to figure out what Robert Chang might be like."

"She always surprised me," Harrison said. "Overall she tended to be on the reserved side, didn't like to stand out, but then she'd come out with a hilarious joke or show up for lunch wearing a bright pink jacket or huge dangling earrings. So she can definitely be a little unpredictable. She's smart, kind, crazy about animals and loves old movies, particularly anything starring Bette Davis. I always had a great time whenever we got together."

She could easily see the sadness that passed over his expression. His aunt Lolly was the only family he had left. "Well, I can see why Robert Chang fell for her. She sounds wonderful. Eclectic."

"I'd like you to meet her," he said, then quickly took a long drink of his iced tea as if he hadn't meant to say that. "I don't know if you should—I mean, based on what you said before about your last name and the connection to Bo and if the memories will upset her."

Daisy gave something of a nod. Harrison was important to her—of course she wanted to meet his dear aunt. But because of this cold-case situation between their fathers, everything was a mess. And up in the air. Daisy hated *up in the air*. "I wish I could meet her. But I don't want to stir up any heartache. Especially not when she'll be reunited with Robert."

"I have a good feeling about inviting Robert to

visit her," he said. "On one hand setting this all up feels weird, but on the other hand, it feels right. It feels *necessary*."

Like you, she thought unbidden, wondering where the hell that had come from. But it was true. He had become necessary. She was in love with the man, trouble or not. Future heartbreak or not, and she had no doubt this was going to get messy. At some point, he'd demand they turn over the ranch. And they weren't about to. Not without a court order.

How could this possibly end well?

Ugh. Now her appetite was disappearing. Luckily, the moment the waiter set down the plates, which smelled so good, her cravings came roaring back and she could hardly wait to take a bite of her sandwich.

"What was your dad's favorite thing to order here?" she asked. Gulp. Maybe that was a mistake. Should she bring up his dad, who'd hated her dad? Whose final wishes were to right the wrong done to him? And to Lolly?

"Every time we came here, he ordered something different. He always got a basket of fries for the table—the fries here are too irresistible not to—but he always ordered a different entrée and a different side."

Daisy smiled. "I love that. Adventurous. My

dad was a creature of habit. Same beer. Same burger joint. He had a favorite Mexican restaurant, too, and went there a few times a week."

Harrison smiled and swiped a fry in ketchup. "I can be like that, too. Tried and true."

"Some people just know what they like," she said.

He held her gaze for a few seconds.

"Can I have a fry?" she asked. "And by a fry, I mean a few."

He laughed. "Help yourself. They definitely give you a ton here."

She heaped a small pile on her plate and dipped a fry into the spicy mayo that came on the side of every plate. "Heavenly," she said.

He glanced up at her. "My dad used to say that while dragging his fries through that very mayo. He loved that mayonnaise and tried to make it at home but never got the proportions right. He'd learned to ask for a few little containers of it to go, and they always obliged. When he was in the hospital right before..." He trailed off and looked down at his plate.

"I'm so sorry, Harrison. I know how much it hurts." She reached across the table and took his hand.

He cleared his throat and pulled his hand away, ostensibly to take a drink of his iced tea, but she could tell he needed some distance. "I went to his condo to pack a bag for him, and there were three containers of the mayo in the fridge. I admit, I broke down. We'd just been here the day before."

"What happened?"

"We were on our way to a cardiologist, actually—just a few blocks from here. My dad had been complaining of chest pain the past few days, and I insisted he ask for an emergency appointment. He grabbed his chest right in the middle of the sidewalk just a block from the medical office. An ambulance came and took him to the ER instead, his doctor hurrying over. He was admitted and monitored, in dire condition."

Her eyes were glistening. "You didn't leave his bedside."

Harrison shook his head. "No, and my aunt was there often, in tears. The final morning, very early, around three or four, Lolly went to get the two of us coffee. We'd been up all night keeping vigil, and that's when my dad told me the story of the bet and Bo Dawson and Lolly."

Daisy glanced down at her plate, willing herself not to burst into tears.

He clearly realized that. "I'm sorry, Daisy," he said, his voice soft. "You're just very easy to talk to, you know?"

She gave a little smile. "I could say the same

about you. Makes me tell you too much." She took a breath and looked at him. "Did you lose your dad right after that?"

"Couple hours. I was seeing red over the bet and the ranch. I kept hearing him say, 'That ranch belongs to us. Get it back.' And that's been burning in my gut ever since."

She suddenly understood how he must feel right now. Sitting in the restaurant that represented his father to him. With Bo Dawson's daughter. Pulled into her grand plan to stop him from fulfilling his dad's dying request.

Daisy could not feel more like dog doo.

But this was not her fault. It wasn't her brothers' fault. The ranch did not belong to the McCords because of a drunken bet. There was supposed to have been a punch in the face—a stupid punch, and it would have ended right there. But it had escalated—Eric McCord insisting on upping the stakes. And so Bo had bet the fallen-down ranch.

There was no way she could say that. Certainly not right now when Harrison's grief was palpable. Bo hadn't been the best dad in the world, and they certainly hadn't been close. His death had still knocked her upside the head, the sorrowful pain of it still catching her to this day, several months later. But from everything Harrison had told her about Eric McCord, he had been dad of the year, they'd been very close and Harrison had just lost him a little over two weeks ago.

She knew his grief was at work in his determination to take ownership of the ranch. Maybe she should just back off from even talking about it? Harrison would need time—deserved time. She of all people knew that.

She stared at her fries for a moment. She wanted Harrison to have what he needed, but what he needed was to make everything okay for his family, to avenge the swindle, and that was something she'd fight him on with every ounce of strength she had.

"You okay?" he asked.

The voice and looking up at his face changed everything. What she and Harrison had, if they had anything, was between them and had nothing to do with the past or her father or his. Something truly special had come out of something hard. It had started on that roadside, and it had blossomed from there without either of them able to stop it. Because it was that strong.

Given how they'd kissed yesterday, that she was sitting right here with him, on this quest to find his aunt's boyfriend, listening to him talk about his father and losing him, Daisy knew she wasn't alone in what she felt.

But what were they going to do about it? He

couldn't walk away from the ranch. How could he? Let his father's last request go unfulfilled? The way he saw it, the ranch really did belong to his father. And despite how he might feel about her and how unfair it was from the Dawson point of view... She shivered in her seat, the air-conditioning suddenly giving her goose bumps. What was she going to do?

"I'm okay," she lied, picking up a fry she had no appetite to eat.

"No, you're not, and neither am I."

She smiled, and he reached his hand across the table.

"Whaddaya say we get home to Tony," he said, and she watched him stiffen.

Daisy herself was frozen in place for a second.

"I mean get you home and me to my cabin," he rushed to add. "Home being the ranch for the next few days for me."

She held on to his hand. "We really are in trouble, Harrison. Let's just call it out. We've got a problem." They knew what it was, and there was no need to talk about it.

"Yeah, we do."

"You like me and I like you," she said.

He nodded. "Yup."

Except for her it went much further than *like*.

* * *

Neither said much on the drive back to Bear Ridge. Daisy called Sara to let her know they'd be back in about twenty minutes, and Sara reported that Tony had been a perfect gentleman the whole time and had spent a lot of his waking hours staring at his comical cousins having their tummy time or in their baby swings. Daisy couldn't wait to get home to see him and hold him and take care of him. She'd missed him so much these past five hours.

When they drove through the gates of the ranch, she waved at Carly, the greeter in the welcome station, which was a hunter-green shed full of creature comforts so Carly wouldn't get bored. Noah liked having a receptionist of sorts at the gate, and so did guests, who always mentioned in their comments online about the ranch that they always felt safe and comfortable coming and going, because someone was always there during business hours (which in ranch terms were seven to seven).

Finally, they'd arrived at the farmhouse. Daisy was glad Harrison didn't turn off the engine and make any moves to come in; they clearly both needed a breather from that whopper of a lunch, some time to think. "How's around six o'clock for the tour of the ranch?" he asked.

Did she even have a tour in her? She wasn't

sure. But she did like the idea of having plans with him. "See you then."

He looked relieved. They were two peas, that was for sure.

She dashed up the porch steps and turned to watch him drive down the road toward the guest cabins. She closed her eyes for a second and sucked in some air, then ran inside.

"Where's my precious boy?" she called out. One was outside driving away—another was in this house.

Sara came into the foyer with a big smile, Tony in her arms. Her sister-in-law carefully transferred him to Daisy.

She could see Annabel and Chance having more tummy time on play mats, each gurgling and happy. "How do you make taking care of three babies look this easy?"

Sara grinned. "Oh, trust me, I had help all morning. Axel was here for a good hour and a half, then Noah came over and we took all three tots for a walk." Her phone pinged, and she pulled it from her back pocket. "Noah. He's waiting for me at our cabin. He's going to be on twin duty while I get back to work."

Just as Sara and the twins were leaving, Axel came in. Which reminded Daisy of the dinner party—that whole thing had gone right out of her head today. And she wanted to keep this plan of hers at the forefront. If she was trying to keep Axel in town, it meant she wasn't putting much stock in the ranch getting swiped out from under them.

Was she delusional? Ignoring reality? Being a total fool? Maybe.

But when Harrison was talking about his dad today, it reinforced how important, how special, family was. Two Dawsons had unexpectedly come home to the ranch to stay. There was a chance for a third right now. How could she not take it and run with it?

With three here, maybe the three scattered across the state would look at the idea differently.

As Axel came over making peekaboo faces at Tony, whom she was holding, she realized a last-minute, very casual invitation to a dinner party would work more in her favor to get a yes out of Axel than some long-planned event. Then she'd just have to pray that Hailey was mysteriously free tomorrow. She knew Hailey was a bit of a home-body when she wasn't working, so there was a good chance.

"Axel, I thought I'd have a few people over to-morrow night," she said. "I'm making my spe-cialty—honey-garlic stir-fry and that delicious rice you love. You'll be there, right?"

"I do love that stir-fry. Count me in." *She* loved

that he didn't ask who else was coming. That was Axel. He wouldn't much care who'd be there. Her brother wasn't exactly a people person. He was a wilderness person. *Like Hailey*, she thought with a happy, inward smile.

Axel made funny faces at Tony, played another few rounds of peekaboo and then told Daisy he was heading upstairs for a shower before helping out with the horseback riding lessons in the main pasture by the big barn. He sure did seem to like working on the ranch, even if he viewed it as temporary.

Maybe *because* he viewed it as temporary.

All she knew was that she had a yes out of him for dinner tomorrow. Now she just needed Hailey to say the same.

She put Tony in his bassinet and grabbed her phone. *Please don't have plans*, she prayed as she dialed. Hailey worked part-time at the ranch but wasn't scheduled to work today.

"Hi, Hailey, it's Daisy Dawson. I'm having a few people over for dinner tomorrow night, and I'd love if you could come."

"Is this a fix up?" Hailey asked on a laugh.

"Is it okay if it is?" *Please say yes. Please say yes.*

"Does it involve your gorgeous brother Axel?" Hailey asked.

"He'll be there. You two sure have a lot in common. He's a search-and-rescue specialist. You lead wilderness tours. You could talk about trails and mountain cliffs for hours, I'll bet."

She was reminded of something Noah once told her when she tried to fix him up with someone years ago, a woman who was a cowgirl through and through like Noah was a cowboy. *Just because you have everything in common doesn't mean you'll have a lick of chemistry. And it's the chemistry that counts.*

He'd turned out to be right about the cowgirl, but Daisy later figured out the real problem with Noah and all the women he'd dated back when was that none of them was Sara, who'd always been the love of his life, even though they'd been apart for years before finally reuniting this past May.

Still, having something big in common had to help with conversation. So she was keeping a very positive view of her matchmaking notions.

Hailey laughed. "I hate fix ups, but I have to say, I have noticed Axel. He's hard to miss."

Axel was a good-looking guy, that was for sure. "I'll see you tomorrow at seven," Daisy said and pocketed her phone. She picked up Tony from his bassinet and gave a triumphant spin. Not only was Hailey free, but she was totally into the setup! Yee-haw!

Axel, you'll soon be madly in love and building that fancy log cabin.

Of course, there might be technical difficulties with that last bit, but right now, that was the fairy tale she had in her head, so she was going with it and forgetting all about where Enemy Hot Stuff fit in.

She had a real chance here for Axel to see that the ranch was part of him, that Bear Ridge didn't have to be about the past, but about the future.

If only she could get that through to the guy she was crazy about in Cabin No. 1.

There was a knock on the door, and Daisy went to see who it was.

"Tessa, hi," Daisy said, noting that the pretty newlywed looked much happier than the last time they'd spoken. Her red cat's-eye sunglasses were atop her head, holding her dark hair off her face. "I was hoping to run into you to ask how things were going."

"Thanks to your advice—a lot better. Tom and I really needed to sit down and talk, put everything out on the table. He doesn't like some of what I had to say. And I didn't like some of what he had to say. But we're working through it. So thanks."

"I'm really happy to hear that, Tessa." Hmm, maybe she should invite Tessa and Tom to the dinner party. An extra couple would make it seem truly more like a dinner party and less like a double date, she just realized. And the Monellos were in a good place. "I'm having a small dinner party here tomorrow night at seven. I'd love to have you and Tom join us."

Tessa beamed. "That would be great! Tom could really use some exposure to older people with life experience."

Hey! Daisy was thirty, not a hundred!

"Great," Daisy said. "See you here at seven. I'm making a stir-fry. Come hungry!"

Tessa smiled and practically skipped away, and Daisy felt good about the invitation. She'd helped a young couple with their love. She'd help her brother *find* love. And as far as she and Harrison were concerned, she wasn't going to think about it.

"I don't know what's going to happen with us or that dumb napkin," she said to Tony, giving him a gentle rock as she moved over to the windows and looked out down the hill toward the cabins. She couldn't see them through the thick cover of trees, but she liked knowing Harrison was down there, probably sitting on the love seat in his cabin and thinking the same thoughts she was.

Namely what they were going to do about their crazy feelings for each other.

Chapter Eleven

"So you've seen the main house," Daisy said as she and Harrison stood in front of it later that night. Harrison was here for his tour, and he was jumping out of his skin. There was so much to say—again—about so much, but neither of them was saying it or wanted to. He had this need, this almost aching desire to be near her, so he'd just focus on that. Actually, scratch that. He shouldn't focus on that.

A mess. This was one hell of a mess.

"Ooh, there's that twinge again," Daisy said, rubbing at her lower back. "I don't know what the heck happened. I bent down to pet Dude earlier and got this little wrenching feeling."

"Uh-oh," Harrison said. "When that happens to me, it can mean a few days of soreness. But you did just have a baby, Daisy. I can drive you to the doc—"

"Eh, I'll hold off for a bit and see how I feel. But talk about great timing. I've got a baby in a carrier strapped to my torso and a dinner party tomorrow night. I'll be bending and twisting every which way getting pots and pans and stuff from the fridge and cabinets tomorrow."

"Tell you what," he said. "Let's start by you putting that contraption on me." He pointed at Tony. "I know he doesn't weigh much, but still."

"Really, you wouldn't mind? Tony loves the carrier, being all snuggly next to a warm, beating heart."

"I don't mind at all." Actually, he wasn't sure about this idea of his, but he'd offered, and now he'd have a baby—Daisy's baby—*this close* to his chest. His beating heart. Which was already too affected by both of them.

She plucked Tony out of the carrier and carefully gave him to Harrison, wincing a bit from the movements. Then while Harrison held Tony awkwardly along one arm, Daisy managed to get the carrier strapped to him, giving it a good yank to make sure it was all latched in place. Then she slid Tony back inside. He glanced down at the little profile. Tony seemed quite content, the little bow lips quirking, his eyes closing.

"Next step," he said, "run inside and take two pain relievers. Maybe we should cancel the tour and you should just rest up."

"Nah. A sore back isn't gonna keep me down. I got through three months of awful morning sickness. I can take a little twingey pain here and there. But I will go take some ibuprofen."

She gingerly walked up the porch steps, one hand rubbing at her lower back. It didn't escape him that he wished he could take her aches and pains away.

He looked down at the baby, putting one hand against the back of the carrier. "This is a first," he whispered to Tony. "And I can't say I ever expected to be wearing an infant on my chest, but here you are."

A surge of…something gripped him in the region of his heart. Protectiveness? He cared about Tony Dawson. Of course he did. He'd helped at his birth. This baby would always be special to him. But the feeling, the sensation was more than just protectiveness.

"Everything I figured would happen once I met your mother has gone topsy-turvy," he added to the baby. "Days before I ever met you on the side of that road, I thought I'd sit your mom and uncle down, tell them what's what, show them the proof and then be on my way—temporarily. I figured I'd be in for a fight. There'd be court involved. And then I'd win and that would be that. Well, a few steps before 'that would be that' haven't exactly worked out like I thought. For instance, I never did get on my way, did I? I'm still here."

Holding you.

Crazy about your mother.

Crazy about this ranch. Simply because it's truly special.

His big mouth had Tony's eyes fluttering open, so Harrison swayed a bit to the left and right to rock the baby back to his nap.

"Your mommy has a backache," he whispered even though he was supposed to let the tot fall back asleep and stop yammering to him. "Do you know who gives great massages? Me. Should I tell her that? I don't know. That probably isn't the best idea." Touching Daisy, intensely kneading her lower back, might drive him off the edge. "We'll see how things go, right, Tony? That's often the answer to everything."

Daisy came down the porch steps. "The meds should kick in soon. Follow me, sir," she said, sweeping her arm out toward the big barn about a quarter mile down the path. "Your tour begins."

They nodded hello and waved to various guests,

some on horseback, some at the petting zoo, the mother and daughter, whose names he forgot, headed toward the creek with fishing gear.

"My dad used to take me and Noah fishing a lot," Daisy said, "and whichever older brother might be around, usually Zeke, who was the last to stop wanting to come at all for weekend visits."

There were so many Dawsons, he forgot who was who. "Zeke—is he the business guy or the one who won't say exactly what he does for a living?"

Daisy smiled. "We truly have zero clue what Zeke's job is. He'll only say it's 'sort of classified,' whatever that means. Government spy?"

"Maybe so. You never know."

"*That* is the truth. You never do." She glanced in the direction of the mother and daughter carrying their gear—poles and tackle boxes. "Our dad would bring us to the creek with our fishing poles—homemade ones. We had real fishing poles once, but one day they all disappeared, and Noah was pretty sure Bo sold them, but he never fessed up to that. So we used whatever cast-off odds and ends we found on the ranch that would make a good substitute, added the bait, and one of us would always get a bite. Sometimes it took a couple hours."

"That's a lot of waiting around for one person to get one fish," he said.

Daisy nodded. "That was back before my dad turned a corner—the wrong way, I mean. He was still halfway attentive and we just wanted his time, you know?"

Harrison knew. His father had been almost too attentive, always wanting to go to the mini golf course or go fishing or take in a game at the local university. Eric McCord liked listening to Harrison talk about what was going on in his life—school, college, work, women. And despite all that attention, Harrison couldn't get enough time with his dad. Eric McCord had been Harrison's favorite person on earth.

"It's amazing how forgiving you are," Harrison said. "You didn't forget, but you did forgive."

"Well, you have to, really, for your own peace of mind," she said. "My dad had some good qualities, and in the end, the very end, he made sure we knew he loved us and cared about us, even if he hadn't always shown it."

"With the letters he left you all," Harrison said. He remembered Daisy talking about them. "He left you your mother's rings."

She nodded. "And he left Sara, his foreman's daughter, her mother's garden plot behind the foreman's cabin. Sara and Noah weren't even speaking at that point, not that my dad would have known that. But Bo Dawson thought of his old foreman's daughter who'd lost her mother at a young age, and he bequeathed her that garden bed."

"Did he keep up the garden?"

Daisy laughed. "You can't be serious."

"Well, it sounded possible based on what you were saying. But yeah, given the condition of the ranch ten years ago, according to my father, your dad didn't keep up anything on this place."

"More like he was a one-man wrecking crew." She shook her head. "I really just want to remember the good stuff at this point. He was kind in the end. That's what I want to focus on."

"He made amends for you," Harrison realized aloud. "Same for your brothers?"

"For Noah, definitely. My dad turned Noah's entire life around without even realizing it. Noah had been following in Bo's footsteps until we inherited this place and my dad's letter to Noah asked him to rebuild the ranch."

He glanced at Daisy. She'd told him this before, but now he had a lot more context for the information, and he understood what a big deal it must have been on many levels. "Sort of like your father's trust and faith in him gave him purpose?"

"And helped him forgive," Daisy said. "Noah let go of a lot. And my other brothers and I wanted to help Noah, so we all rallied around the idea of rebuilding the ranch. Having a reopening. Giving my grandparents back their hard work and us the legacy they'd meant to leave us with."

And now she was working on bringing all her brothers home. Part of him—a huge part—wanted her to succeed. Part of him—the part still very focused on his father's last request of Harrison—knew she wasn't going to.

Something in his chest twisted, and now it was him wincing. How could he do that to Daisy?

But how could he avoid it?

Move along, he told himself. *Change the subject in your head.* He looked at the big red barn, the wrought iron weather vane with its rooster on top. There were sheep in one pasture and goats in another. Farther down, at the stables, he could see a ranch hand going down the line of half-open stalls, giving each horse an apple slice.

"Ranch tradition?" Harrison asked, nodding up ahead.

Daisy smiled. "Yup. They get their apples two times a week and carrots two times a week. For dealing with city slickers and people who'd never been on a horse."

"The stories the horses could tell," he said. He could just imagine.

"Yup. So I'm glad they can't talk. But we keep a very careful eye. Even when our guests are out riding, a couple of us are always patrolling for their safety, and the horses', too."

Tony let out a little whine, and they stopped walking to see what was up with the little guy.

"Maybe someone needs a back rub," he said, giving the baby pats through the material of the carrier.

"Yeah, me," she said, giving her own back a rub. "It's a little better, but I can still feel a knot."

Let me at it, he thought. Maybe when they got back to her house, he'd suggest it.

Tony let out a burp, and they both laughed.

"You're pretty good at this," she said, stepping closer to peer at Tony.

"No one is more surprised than me. But Tony and I have a bond, right, buddy?" he said to the baby.

He felt her looking at him, and he kept his gaze straight ahead, once again worried he'd said the wrong thing. Or the right thing. Because if they had a bond, he couldn't possibly take away Tony's future, Tony's legacy, Tony's family history.

"I had my first kiss right behind that little barn," she said, pointing up ahead at the lemon-yellow structure that housed the petting zoo animals. He'd never been so grateful for a change of subject. Out front, in a large pen, a bunch of little goats were grazing, and some were standing on stumps, the youngest guests staring in awe and giggling. "We were both thirteen and so awkward. His name was Charlie, and I was nuts about him. We were a couple for a whole two and a half weeks in eighth grade. He became a fancy state legislator and didn't even acknowledge me when I passed him in town a few months ago. Snob."

"Considering your kisses are unforgettable, he clearly is a snob. Hopefully he'll be voted out next term."

Daisy laughed, then bit her lip and turned to look directly at him. "I haven't been able to forget kissing you, either. I've tried, too. Hard."

"Yeah, same here."

"That's probably why we're getting so close," she said. "We're going through the same thing. Ba-dum-ch!" she added, slapping her thigh. "Not that it's a joke," she added quite seriously. "It's true."

"I know," he said, wanting to take her in his arms more than anything. Luckily, he had a baby against his chest who'd get squished, so he'd keep his hands to himself.

She took a breath and glanced around, then pointed at the gate to the small barn. "Oh—and right here, Skippy Peterman asked me to the junior prom. I was also nuts about him."

"What did Skippy Peterman end up being?" he asked.

"A big-animal veterinarian. That's all he ever wanted to be from the time he could talk."

"And what did young Daisy Dawson want to be?"

She shrugged. "I was always so envious when friends would talk about their dreams and plans. I had no idea what I wanted to do with my life. I guess I just fell into jobs, and none of them really interested me. Once I even worked as a research assistant for a private investigator in Prairie City. You wouldn't believe half of what his clients hired him to do. One guy in the middle of an awful divorce wanted to find his old girlfriend from middle school, and we thought, *this is not going to end well.* We found the woman, and she couldn't even remember the client. She was happily married with four kids."

"What was your favorite job?" he asked as they continued walking past the petting zoo.

"You might not believe this, but it was being a ranch hand here. My grandparents hired me at one dollar an hour when I was seven—their rate for grandchildren depended on age. Every year I got a dollar raise. My first job was mucking out the sheep pen, and I adored those furry bleating creatures so much that I was happy to care for them."

"So you didn't keep on being a hand?"

She shook her head. "When I turned eighteen,

it was just me, Noah, who was sixteen, and my dad left on the ranch. I wanted to escape, get away from my father. I felt so terrible leaving Noah here, but he was so rough around the edges back then I guess I wanted to get away from him, too." She frowned, and her eyes got misty. "I thought college would give me options, but I just floundered. Want to know a secret? I didn't even graduate."

He stopped walking, and so did she. He reached up a hand to her face. "Jobs don't make you who you are, Daisy. Neither does a degree. You're one of the finest people I've ever met."

"Why do you have to be damned nice and always say the right thing?" she asked, a small smile finally appearing on her beautiful face.

"Just comes easy with you. And I mean everything I say."

The smile faded some. He knew she was thinking about how he'd said, multiple times, that he intended to fight for the ranch.

"Well, you've gotten half the grand tour of the ranch, Harrison. I should go lie down, rest my weary back."

"And you want some space," he said.

She nodded.

"I'll walk you home and put Tony in his bassinet for you so you don't have to bend."

"I appreciate that."

They turned around and started heading back toward the main house. Both were quiet, Daisy lifting up her face to the sun, Harrison's mind churning in many directions. He was so aware of the baby against his chest, of the woman beside him.

"Oh no, there goes Hermione again," Daisy said, pointing up toward where the land sloped to a hill. A brown-and-white goat was practically galloping from the pasture. "She keeps getting away, despite how strong Noah makes the enclosure."

"She sure is fast." He glanced down at Tony's sleeping face. "Hey, Tony, you're missing the runaway goat. It's like a cartoon in front of your eyes."

Daisy laughed. "Did I ever tell you that a runaway goat is why Axel became a search-and-rescue specialist?"

"Nope," he said. "I would have remembered that." Harrison pictured tall, muscular Axel Dawson and his brooding stare while giving Harrison the evil eye. Only one Dawson didn't want to chase *him* off the ranch. Make that two. Tony liked having Harrison around.

"When Axel was around eight years old, maybe nine," Daisy said as they continued to walk, "his favorite goat ran off, just like Hermione. Back then, my grandparents would let us name the baby goats, and part of our jobs was to care for the goat we named. So Axel named Flash, and that reddish-gold goat was as good as his name and took off so fast one night when a kid guest left the pen open that no one could catch him. Axel saw it happen and ran after him, but Flash was gone up in the hills toward Clover Mountain."

"Please tell me this ends well," Harrison said. "I need one happy ending."

Daisy smiled. "No spoilers. Well, my grandparents were older then and couldn't go traipsing after Flash. And my dad was the cowboy on duty that night, so he wasn't supposed to leave, but he called in one of the ranch employees and paid him a small fortune to cover for him. My dad took Axel up into the hills and into Clover Mountain, and after two hours of looking, there was no sign of Flash."

Uh-oh, Harrison thought. "So it doesn't end well?"

"Hey, I said no spoilers! Well, there are lots of foxes and coyotes on the mountain, and my dad was sure Flash was gone for good. But they'd dressed right for the trip, both had their fleece hoodies and hats with the headlamps, and Flash's favorite treats, peaches and sunflower seeds to lure him, so they weren't leaving the mountain without the goat—no matter what. Now this was about twenty-three, twenty-four years ago, and we didn't have cell phones. So there was no way to get in touch with my dad. When they weren't back by midnight, my grandfather called the sheriff for help, and the sheriff called his brother, who was a search-and-rescue specialist."

"For that mountain specifically?" Harrison asked.

"Nah, Clover Mountain's summit isn't very far to hike, but there are a lot of twisty trails. Gramps was afraid my dad might have been drinking, despite saying he hadn't, and gotten hurt, leaving little Axel to fend for himself. But the sheriff's brother got a team and went up into the mountain, and guess what they found?"

He grimaced. "Please tell me they found your father, your brother and Flash all sitting around a campfire, roasting marshmallows and telling ghost stories."

Daisy grinned. "Not quite. But—turns out that about halfway up the mountain, Flash had gotten himself trapped on a ledge that they couldn't get to. Axel, only eight, was a wreck. Axel refused to leave the goat, so my dad said they'd wait it out, that help would eventually come, since that was the Dawson way. And finally, at one thirty in the morning, the cavalry arrived. The sheriff's brother used a special pulley thing to get Flash onto the trail. Axel gave Flash a piece of peach and threw his arms around him, then hugged my dad, then the search-and-rescue guy, then the sheriff, who wasn't too happy about having to climb even an easy mountain at that hour."

Harrison threw his hands up. "Thank you, Universe, for the happy ending."

Daisy laughed. "Well, when they got to their vehicles, the sheriff radioed in and had someone call my grandmother, who was beside herself. And we were all awake and waiting when the trucks came in, Flash leaping out on his lead. My gramps strengthened that pen, and Flash never did get away again. And that's why Axel became a search-and-rescue guy. Because he never forgot how he felt when Flash was lost. Or when people cared that he was. And when people rescued him."

He stopped by the porch steps. "I'm glad for Flash and for Axel and for all of you." He thought of the photo he'd seen of Bo Dawson, a tall and rangy cowboy in a Stetson, with a way-too-easy smile and flashing blue eyes, and imagined him parking himself on the mountain at midnight after hours of searching for the goat because his eight-year-old son was sobbing over the idea of leaving Flash there to get eaten by a coyote while they went for help. The more Harrison heard about Bo Dawson, the more he realized he truly did have a good side. Maybe even equal to the bad side. Which was saying something.

"Well," Daisy said, "now we know how long it

is from the petting zoo to the main house—one very long story."

Harrison smiled. "It was a good story." He followed her up the porch steps. "I'll just put Tony in his bassinet and let you rest."

Please say, "Or you can come in and give me a back massage, sailor."

She didn't say that. And he didn't suggest it.

They went inside, and Harrison found himself very reluctantly taking Tony from the carrier and setting him in the bassinet. He missed that soft weight against him, the subtle scent of baby shampoo. He could not for the life of him figure out how to undo all the latches on the baby carrier, so Daisy did that, standing so close to him he could move half an inch and be kissing her.

But then the carrier was off and she was putting it in a basket by the door, and he had no reason not to trail her there on his way out.

And then a really bad-for-his-head-and-heart idea occurred to him, and he blurted it out before he could stop himself. "So how about if I help you out with the dinner party prep tomorrow?" he asked. "You can sit and direct me, and I'll do all the heavy lifting and twisting and bending."

She tilted her head and stared at him, and he could see she was touched. And thinking. Deciding. She gave her lower back a rub, which must have made the decision for her, because she said, "That's really thoughtful of you, Harrison. Everyone's coming at seven, and I'll need a solid forty-five minutes to prep and cook—for *you* to prep and cook—so how about you arrive at five forty-five and we'll get right to it?"

"Do you need anything from the grocery store? I don't mind driving over and picking up anything."

"Could you stop being so thoughtful? And no, I've got everything. But thank you. You're a peach—like the one Axel gave Flash when he was rescued."

His aunt Lolly always used to call him a peach every time he did something nice for her. For once, though, the thought of Lolly was just a sweet one instead of making him all knotted up. "See you tomorrow at five forty-five, then," he said and dragged himself out the door.

As he headed back down to his cabin, he thought about sitting across from her in Franny's Fish and Chips, telling her all about the day he'd lost his dad. How his father told him about Bo and the bet and Lolly. Harrison hadn't understood why he'd told Daisy all that. Not to hurt her, certainly. Or even to make her understand.

But he got it now. He'd told her because he was in love with her. Crazy in love. There was no denying it or trying to ignore it. He'd wanted to share with her—and he'd gone *way* overboard.

Now, *she* was sharing—much more than when they'd first made their deal. Her willingness to be so vulnerable shook him at times—quite a few times the past hour alone. He wasn't sure if she was being so open because she felt the same way he did and wanted to bring him inside her world. *Or* if she really was still working on her grand plan to sway him against taking the ranch. They'd both come clean that they had feelings for each other. So maybe the plan had gone out the window.

He had a feeling they were way past that.

Chapter Twelve

Since Daisy's sister-in-law was working tonight while her husband would be home with their twins, Sara had kindly asked Noah to babysit Tony since he was in baby mode anyway. Sara wholeheartedly approved of the plan to entice Axel into sticking around Bear Ridge and hopefully on the ranch, so she'd casually mentioned to her husband that Daisy "might be fixing up Axel" at a small dinner party. Knowing Noah would not want to know a detail more and that he'd agree just to not get involved, Sara had gotten Daisy a top-notch sitter for Tony, as Noah had taken care of a newborn on his own for seven weeks before

Sara had arrived at the ranch and changed his entire world.

The doorbell rang, and when Daisy opened it, she almost swooned. Standing there was gorgeous, sexy Harrison in black chinos and a black polo shirt, looking as mysterious as he'd seemed the day she'd met him. In one hand he had a huge bouquet of pink flowers, and in the other a little shopping bag from Heavenly Bake, which he held out to her. She peeked in to find a delicious-looking round loaf of crusty bread from the excellent small bakery right in town.

Daisy felt so underdressed in her yoga shorts and a flowy tank top. She planned to change for dinner once everything was all set. She could hardly take her eyes off Harrison. Even speaking was beyond her for the moment, but she managed to thank him for the flowers and bread.

"You sit," he said, pointing at the upholstered red velvet armchair in the corner by the window. "I'm at your service." He took one of the three stained glass vases on the counter and filled it with water, then put in the flowers, even giving them a little arranging before setting the vase on the kitchen table. "I'll bring these into the dining room later."

She smiled and sat, the twinge in her back still nipping, but it was better than earlier. "The flowers are gorgeous," she said, admiring them. "And this was Gram's chair, if you were wondering why a living room chair is in the kitchen. She would plonk down in it while something cooked or baked so she could keep watch." She rubbed her hands over the arms. "It reminds me of her, so I kept it here. I think it brings me luck."

"Well, if I don't burn dinner," he said, "we'll know it really does."

He seriously had to stop making her adore him. She eyed his clothes and realized he'd better wear an apron. "You look way too nice to risk getting splattered with chicken- and garlic-scented sesame oil. You can wear my apron—hanging on that peg." She pointed at the wall.

He put it on, tying it around his waist. He glanced down at himself. "'Baby on Board,'" he read aloud. "I guess this apron is only true for nine months at most."

"Yup. It was a gift from Noah when I first came back to the ranch. Hey, it was true for you during the tour earlier. You had a baby on board." She smiled, despite being aware that the memory of him walking around with Tony strapped to his chest would haunt her every night forever.

"Hey, where is the little guy? Upstairs sleeping?"

She shook her head. "Noah's on baby duty tonight while Sara works, so he's watching Tony, too. He's great with babies."

"Does he know I'm here?"

She gave a half shrug. "I told Sara, so I'm sure he knows."

"And what does the foreman of the Dawson Family Guest Ranch, the man who rebuilt this place, think of you cavorting with the enemy? He and Axel must not think it's too wise."

"They don't," she said. "But they know it's all part of my plan to change your mind by making you crazy about us, so they're grudgingly accepting it."

He let out a breath. He sure was crazy about Daisy. And everything he knew about her brothers had him respecting them immensely. But his mind was far from changed. It was more temporarily stalled—as in he wasn't going to focus on it until he had to. The five days weren't up. A deal was a deal.

"Okay, less chitchat, more cooking!" she said in her best drill sergeant tone. "I printed out a copy of my recipe for you. It's on the counter. You sure you want to do everything yourself?"

"Yup." He scanned the recipe and instructions. "So it's the four of us, right? This looks like it'll feed a small army."

"Actually, it's six. Remember the newlyweds,

Tessa and Tom Monello? We saw them making out on the path the other day. I invited them, too. They're having issues, and I kind of helped Tessa with a little advice—not that I know anything about marriage, but my advice seems to have helped. She came to tell me yesterday, and I ended up inviting them. I think Axel will feel it's less like a double date that way."

He stared at her. "Is that how you saw it? A double date?"

Well, when he put it like *that*. "Well, no, of course not. We're not dating."

"I know, but we're *something*, Daisy."

"Yes, we're something. But we're not dating. Or friends," she added with a smile.

All I know is that I love you, she thought, wishing she could scream it from the rooftops. Wishing she could know what the hell was going to happen when all was said and done.

"Speaking of dating, have you heard back from Robert Chang, by any chance?" She really should let the chef get busy, but she was dying to know.

He shook his head. "I'm figuring he'll call back tomorrow when he's had a chance to settle back in and digest the news that Lolly's nephew wants to talk to him. I really hope that doesn't blow up in my face."

She nodded. "I feel that way about tonight."

"Well, I can promise you I'll follow your recipe to the T, so at least your famed stir-fry and special recipe rice should still manage to wow the crowd."

"I wouldn't go that far," she quipped as he started pulling out pots and bowls and utensils. He went to the fridge and got out all the vegetables for the stir-fry and eyed the knives in the block on the counter.

"Second one down is great for fine chopping," she said.

"Oh wait, I should probably get the rice going first, right?"

She nodded, mesmerized by the sight of him in her apron, zooming about her kitchen. She wished she could take a photo. Oh hell, why not. Her cell phone was right in her pocket. "I'll get a photo of you hard at work on the recipe, your ingredients all around you," she said super casually, as if she just didn't want a photo to remember him by before things went really south. And they would, she knew. There was no other way for the situation to go.

He turned, holding the big glass jar of rice that she kept on the counter, surrounded by broccoli and snap peas and mushrooms and carrots. "Cheese," he said, and she laughed and snapped the photo. She'd ogle it later.

Once the rice was going, he started chopping

away, maybe chopping the broccoli a little too much, concentrating so hard on what he was doing that she stayed quiet and just watched him. He did great with the mushrooms.

"I'll make the sauce," she said, getting up and realizing she did so without reaching for her lower back. "Hey, the twinge is gone. I think whatever knot that was worked itself out. Last night's hot bath and spending most of today lying on the sofa with Tony must have helped."

"Glad to hear it. But I still want to cook. One wrong reach and you could reinjure whatever you pulled. I'll collect what you need for sauce, though, and you can make it from the table."

My hero, she thought. She watched him read over the ingredients, then get out the garlic and ginger and sesame oil and everything else. He brought it all to the table, leaning over so close that she could reach up and kiss his cheek, which she wanted to do. He brought over the knife block, a chopping board and one of the dish towels, and she was so overwhelmed by his nearness and his thoughtfulness and his sexiness that she stood up and took his face and kissed him. Really kissed him—on the lips.

He kissed her right back. She leaned him against the counter, vaguely aware that she was glad she hadn't yet touched the garlic, because her hands were all over the part of his shirt not covered by the apron. Then in his hair. He held her so close, and she felt the most wonderful sensation of desire and safety and pure happiness.

She barely heard the front door opening and closing. Work boots being kicked off in the foyer.

"Daize?" Axel's voice rang out. "Need help with dinner?"

Double drat. She pulled away. Harrison stepped back just as Axel came into the kitchen.

"Oh," Axel said, giving Harrison the usual stare of death. "Guess you have help."

"You're a guest tonight," she told Axel, "so go relax. Come down at seven. I invited Hailey Appleton, by the way. And the newlywed guests—the Monellos. Know them?"

"Why'd you invite Hailey?" Axel asked, narrowing his gaze at her.

"I realized I hadn't gotten a chance to talk to her in a while even though she's often right here on the ranch, so I figured I'd just ask her to dinner. Lucky Hailey was free since I asked her so last minute." Not a word of that was a lie. And it seemed to soothe Axel away from thinking she was trying to fix him up with Hailey.

"If you need any help, let me know," Axel said, eyeing Harrison before leaving the kitchen.

Harrison glanced at her, then turned back to the recipe. "I feel lucky I'm still alive."

She smiled. "Well, the situation is what it is, as they say. Axel and Noah are very, very wary of you. They don't love what I've been trying to do—trying to get you to like us so much that you'll just disappear."

He turned and looked at her. "Is that what you want, Daisy? For me to disappear?"

"What I want is for you to rip up the napkin," she said, wondering if she should be really honest and say the rest of the sentence out loud. She hesitated, then added, "And then *not* disappear."

"So I rip up the napkin or it's see ya." He stood stock-still, and she really hoped he didn't walk out.

Tears pricked her eyes out of nowhere. "This is really hard, Harrison. What do you expect me to do or say? The ranch is everything to me and my family."

He turned back to the counter, where vegetables were awaiting the pan. "Let's get back to cooking. Your guests are coming in forty minutes."

She nodded, relieved he was staying, but her stomach was all twisty now. He went to the fridge and got out the chicken, and for the next ten minutes, neither of them said a word.

Finally, he asked her a question about when to turn the chicken, and that kind of broke the ice since she got up to look, and then they were back to chatting away about light stuff, like the time her brother Rex accidentally fell on her with an open-faced peanut-butter sandwich that landed hard on her head. They laughed and traded funny stories, but the tension never left either of their voices, and Harrison's shoulders never quite relaxed.

And she thought the two of them would be the anchors of the dinner party? Oh boy.

"Ooh, this is delicious!" Hailey said after taking her first bite of stir-fry.

Harrison grinned. "I'm very, very relieved. I did the cooking from Daisy's recipe."

"It's not bad," Axel said with a nod.

Harrison would take that as high praise. He and Daisy sat at either end of the rectangular table in the dining room as if they were married and this were their house, the Monellos across from each other on his side, and the would-be couple on Daisy's end. The flowers he'd brought were in the center, along with the bread, which he'd sliced. The stir-fry and rice were on a big platter, and he was glad to see that everyone was eating heartily. He hadn't burned any part of dinner, and Daisy, who still seemed a bit strained, had told him everything was perfect. Food-wise, she'd added.

As Axel took a slice of the bread, Harrison noticed Hailey looking at him—with interest. Harrison couldn't get a read on Axel at all. He'd been polite since he came down, offering to set the table, but Harrison had already taken care of that. Axel had offered him one of his favorite craft beers, which Harrison had accepted, but there was no clinking of bottles. Harrison had never seen Axel out of his ranch duds, but now he was in dark gray pants with a pale gray collared shirt. Hailey wore a sundress, her red hair long and loose. Daisy looked stunning in her own sundress, hers white with tiny straps and embroidered with little flowers along the hem and neckline. The Monellos were decked out for a nightclub.

"So, Hailey," Daisy said, pushing stir-fry around her plate. "Noah mentioned you're taking all the guests out on a wilderness tour tomorrow up into Clover Mountain. That's great that all the cabins signed up—even the youngest kids are going."

"I was so happy to see the sign-up sheet," Hailey said, her brown eyes glowing. "Many times the guests really just want to relax or take a quick hike up the creek."

"You'll have a partner, right?" Axel asked, his gaze on Hailey.

Hailey took a sip of her wine. "Yup. Dylan, the ranch hand, will be assisting."

Axel nodded. "Good. Better to have two skilled

trail leaders with a group that size, particularly with kids."

"Oh I know," Hailey said. "My toddler can dash away so fast, and he's only eighteen months! One second he's there, the next I find him playing hide-and-seek in the coat closet, scaring me to death."

Daisy hadn't mentioned that Hailey had a child. Harrison glanced at her, and she looked surprised. He then eyed Axel, who was sitting as ramrod straight as Harrison had been earlier when all that tension had flared up between himself and Daisy in the kitchen. Interesting.

"See!" Tom Monello said to his wife, his hazel eyes triumphant. He then looked at Hailey. "You're what, twenty-five? And already have a toddler. You and your husband are probably already planning the next baby when the little one turns two, am I right?"

Hailey lifted her chin. "Actually, I'm not married. So it's just me and Jonathan."

"Oh," Tom said.

"That was a lot to assume," Tessa said to her husband through gritted teeth. She shoved her long dark wavy hair behind her shoulders, her eyes flashing.

Tom shrugged. "But she started young. Now she has time to find a new husband and have another kid."

"Um, Tom, seriously!" Tessa snapped. "I'm so sorry—uh, what was your name again? Bailey?"

Hailey turned bright red. "It's Hailey."

Daisy looked mortified and like she was clamping down on saying what was bursting inside her. "More stir-fry, anyone?"

No one seemed to hear her. Axel was staring at his plate and pushing rice around. Hailey had that deer-in-headlights look. Tessa seemed about to stab her husband with her fork. And Tom was busily eating.

Tom finally put down his fork, then sipped his beer. "I'm just saying, Tessa. If we start having kids now, we can have three by the time we're thirty. That's ideal."

"According to whom?" Daisy asked.

"His mother," Tessa said.

Daisy's expression said she was sorry she'd asked. "So, Axel," she said brightly, turning her attention to her brother. "Back to the wilderness tour Hailey's leading tomorrow. Are you free to join them?" she asked. Very casually.

Despite the bickering going on at Harrison's end of the table, you could hear a pin drop at Daisy's side. Axel and Hailey were both dead silent.

Daisy seemed to be holding her breath.

Axel glanced at Hailey, then at Daisy, then sort of at the two of them. "I'll have to check my calendar. I'm going to an auction with Noah tomorrow, but I'm not sure of the time."

"I'd love for you to join us," Hailey said, but her voice was a little unsteady. "I've been leading tours a long time, but a search-and-rescue specialist could give a great talk at our rest stops about hazards. Plus, we really could use the extra set of eagle eyes."

Axel nodded. "I'll let you know in the morning. I'll get your number from Daisy."

Hailey seemed to perk up a bit at that. But if someone took a photo of the dinner party guests right now, there wouldn't be a smile on any face.

Harrison glanced at Daisy. She did seem about half-pleased. Half that there was a potential get-together on the table. Half that Axel had seemed so…lackluster about it. Of course, that could just be his way.

Tessa stood. "Daisy, thank you so much for inviting us. Everything was delicious. But we actually have to get going."

Tom grudgingly stood, then took one more bite of stir-fry. And then finished his piece of bread. "You said we should say what we feel, what we want," he complained. "That's what I'm doing. Suddenly I'm the bad guy?"

"But what you want is not what I want!" Tessa said, tears glistening.

This wasn't going well.

"Well, what you want isn't what I want," Tom said, crossing his arms over his chest.

"Guys, look," Daisy said, standing up. "You two love each other. You do know that, right? You love each other. If you each want something different, you're going to have to learn to compromise."

Tessa glared at her. "Um, Daisy, no offense, but this is kind of personal, so…"

Harrison could see Daisy was fighting not to roll her eyes. Hard. "But Daisy is right. You're either at a stalemate and it tears you apart. Or you compromise and it brings you together because you had to work together to get there."

"I guess," Tom said—grudgingly.

"Let's go," Tessa said. "None of these people are even *married*," he heard Tessa mutter under her breath to her husband, who scowled at Daisy and Harrison before putting his arm around his wife's shoulder.

"We'll walk you out," Harrison said, getting up, too.

He and Daisy led the way to the front door, and then finally the Monellos were headed up the trail toward their cabin.

Daisy let out a long breath. As guest relations manager, maternity leave or not, she'd have to smooth things out with them in the morning, and

she would. For the sake of the ranch and their online reviews.

"Think they'll make it to Christmas?" Harrison asked.

"Yes, actually," Daisy said. "They're immature
and young, but they do love each other. I honestly
think they'll bicker their way to their sixtieth wedding anniversary."

"A romantic like me," Hailey called out. "And I
agree. Tom and Tessa were in my tour group a couple days ago, and they had three arguments within
a half hour. The way back—they never stopped
kissing. How they didn't trip was beyond me."

Axel laughed. "I actually did see them trip yesterday—well, more like walk right into a half stone
wall. They were lip-locked and *bam*—suddenly
both rubbing their knees."

"I'm sure they kissed each other's boo-boos,"
Hailey said on a chuckle, but then her eyes widened and two splotches of pink appeared on her
cheeks.

"No doubt," Axel said, lifting his beer to Hailey.
She lifted hers back with a happy smile.

And just like that, this dinner party was back
in business. Daisy brought out three desserts—
starting with the coffee cake the Monellos had
brought. His aunt had always loved that brand of
coffee cake, and Harrison had had many a slice in

his lifetime. He would definitely partake tonight. Hailey had brought a homemade peach pie, one of Harrison's favorite kinds. And Daisy had baked chocolate chip cookies. Harrison got up to make a pot of coffee as if this was his house—a thought that only occurred to him after Axel glared at him.

This *would* be his house. Now that was a thought that sobered him up real fast. He stood in the kitchen, staring at the coffee dripping into the decanter, his collar tightening on him. He was going to take Daisy's house? Tony's house?

Daisy came into the kitchen, and he tried to shake off how unsettled he felt. "I'll get the cream and sugar. Leaving Axel and Hailey alone for a bit seems a great idea about now," she whispered with a smile.

"You might have had to suffer through the Monellos," he said, "but this dinner party seems to have served its purpose."

"I hope so. I have a good feeling."

A few minutes later, they brought in the coffee, and they all dug into dessert, swapping stories. Hailey had everyone in stitches about the antics of her little dog, a beagle mix whom her toddler adored. Then Axel told the tale of trying to hide a huge stray dog on the ranch for a week when he was a little kid. His grandparents wouldn't allow dogs and arranged for their closest neighbors to adopt the giant stray, and they'd hired Axel to be their daily dog walker and afternoon feeder, so it had all worked out. Hailey was beaming. Axel seemed relaxed and happy. Daisy was thrilled.

On cue, as if he knew they were talking dogs, Dude came over to the table and put his chin right on Harrison's lap.

"Aww," Hailey said. "Dude sure does like you, Harrison."

Axel scowled, staring at his yellow Lab, then at Harrison. "Yeah, a little too much for comfort."

Daisy bit her lip.

"Am I missing something?" Hailey asked, looking between Axel and Harrison.

All eyes swung to Axel. Harrison looked down at sweet Dude with a sigh.

"Yes," Axel said, "but be glad you are, because it's ugly. Really ugly."

Hailey looked confused. Daisy looked nervous. Axel looked ready to punch the wall.

And Harrison figured he'd better leave, give Daisy a chance to calm things down, save the night for her brother and Hailey.

Axel glared at Harrison. "How the hell can you sit there and eat our food, laugh at our stories, and do what you're planning to do? How the hell can you? I think you should leave."

"I think so, too," Harrison said, standing up. "This was a nice night. I don't want to ruin it."

"Harrison," Daisy said. "Wait—"

"Yes, wait," Axel said suddenly. "I have an idea."

He stared at Daisy's brother. It clearly wasn't an idea that made the guy any less angry.

Axel rounded the table and stood inches from Harrison. "Hit me. Punch me square in the face like your father was supposed to do to my father. Then we'll be even. That was the original payment, right? A knockout. The bet came later when Bo Dawson was drunk off his keister. It's why he lost the poker game, by the way. So hardly fair. Hit me and rip up the napkin."

Harrison looked at Daisy, who bolted up and rushed over.

"No one is punching anyone!" she shouted.

"Um, I think I'd better get going," Hailey said and practically ran out the door.

Daisy threw up her hands. "Great. Now the fix up is ruined! Great going, guys!"

"Wait—you were fixing me up with Hailey?" Axel asked.

"Duh!" Daisy said. "Now she thinks we're people who go around screaming and yelling and fist-fighting and sending newlyweds running for the hills."

"I'm sorry this didn't go the way you'd hoped, Daisy," Harrison said, so heavyhearted he was surprised he didn't crash through the floor. He turned to Axel. "I understand why you're so angry, Axel. I do. I wish things were different, but they're not."

Daisy's eyes glistened as she stared at Harrison. "*What?* Are you telling me you're actually *really* still planning to take the ranch from us? Try to, I should say. Because you won't! No court will agree with you!"

That heavy heart of his split in two. He turned and walked to the front door. With his hand on the doorknob, he turned to look at Daisy, to implore her to understand—as if she could. But she was sobbing against her brother, who was hugging her protectively and telling her they'd fight Harrison—in court—with everything they had. And they had a lot.

They did. The six Dawsons had one another.

Chapter Thirteen

Daisy hadn't slept much last night, but she was out cold when Tony's cries from the nursery made their way into her brain from the baby monitor on her bedside table. She eyed the clock—6:14 a.m. She'd been up with Tony just after three and had finally fallen asleep at right before four. No wonder she was bleary-eyed.

Oh, and the crying she'd done.

She shoved off the quilt and went into the nursery, the sight of her baby boy making her so happy she forgot how exhausted she was and cuddled him against her. "How about a change and then some breakfast, my sweet?"

Once he was changed and dressed in a cute blue-and-green onesie with stretchy shorts, she headed downstairs for the coffeepot. Why she thought two or three mugs of decaf would wake her up was beyond her, but drinking hot coffee always faked her brain.

With Tony in his bassinet, she made the coffee and toasted a sesame seed bagel, getting out the cream cheese, which of course reminded her of Harrison.

He'd been all over this fridge last night. So helpful. So wonderful.

And then blammo. The whole thing had come crashing down on her head, which it could have done at any moment. Last night had just been pushed along by Axel—something that needed to happen so she'd wake up and actually smell the coffee. Which she literally and figuratively did right now.

The plan to make Harrison like them had worked. He liked them. No one doubted that.

The plan itself? Did not work. Had no effect on the outcome. He was still going to try to take the ranch from them. She should have seen that coming, but she'd been too blinded by a pair of intense green eyes and the tousled, sexy blond hair and the great jawline. And the great body. And the great kissing.

She grabbed a mug from the cabinet and poured her coffee, adding cream and sugar, and then took a satisfying few sips. The heat helped clear her mind even if the lack of caffeine meant no boost.

She sat down with her bagel and coffee, watching Tony stare at his gently spinning pastel mobile with the little farm animals. At least she was all cried out. Axel had let her sob all over his shirt last night after Harrison had left. Dude had felt so bad for her he'd lain at her feet, his chin on her foot.

Well, Daisy had to admit that Harrison McCord's presence on the ranch—and in her life— had actually managed to bring her and Axel closer, so that was a major positive. When she'd finally stopped crying, she and Axel had gone onto the back deck with Dude and they'd talked for a long time. Daisy had told him everything. How the plan had never gone off track, exactly, but that she'd actually managed to fall madly in love with the guy.

Because he was her brother and he loved her, Axel had said that if Harrison McCord weren't trying to ruin their lives, he'd be a great guy. Axel had even admitted to finding himself forgetting who Harrison actually was during dinner and enjoying the conversation—when it hadn't gone off the rails in some way or another.

She and Axel had been up past midnight talking about the ranch. Axel had told her that, like their brothers, who'd been talking about the "McCord Problem," as they called it, the threat of losing the ranch had made them realize that they actually cared much more about the place than they'd understood. They'd thought it was about their grandparents, their hard work, their family legacy. But it was much more. It was about *now*. It was about all six Dawsons rallying and investing in rebuilding the ranch. About Noah coming into his own while renovating. About Daisy finding a safe place to land when she was pregnant and felt so alone. About the future they'd created and were creating for the next generation.

"I won't start building that fancy log cabin until a judge orders McCord to rip up that napkin," Axel had said. "But I'm not going anywhere."

Her heart had soared at that. One mission accomplished. They weren't going to lose the ranch because they were Dawsons, dammit, and she wasn't going to lose Axel. He was staying. He'd even promised to apologize to Hailey when he texted her about whether or not he could go on the wilderness tour with her.

She had lost Harrison, though. Whatever they'd had—and they did have something truly special—was over. If he could actually try to steal the ranch out from under them, he wasn't the man she thought he was. His father's last request or not. It wasn't a fair request.

"I don't know if that's fair of *me*," she said to Tony. "But it's how I feel."

Daisy looked at the baby boy in the bassinet, his gaze moving to hers. She had her precious son. She had her family. She had this ranch. That would get her through, heart imploding and exploding all over the place.

Harrison was holed up in the cabin, trying to figure out what the hell to do. Last night, since he'd spent hours tossing and turning and not getting any sleep, he'd vowed to stay at the ranch instead of hightailing it back to Prairie City before five Dawson brothers came after him. He had today and tomorrow left on his stay at the ranch. On the deal, too. He wasn't leaving. Not when everything was so awful between him and Daisy.

He needed to go see Lolly. If she was sleeping, he'd gently wake her and ask her what she thought he should do about the ranch. He wouldn't tell her about falling for Daisy. He'd just ask her what she wanted. If the ranch belonged to anyone right now, in his eyes, it was Lolly. It hadn't passed from his father to him—it went to his aunt, then to him. That was how Harrison viewed it. He'd get his cues from Lolly. Then go from there.

His phone rang, and he lunged for it, hoping it was Daisy. But it was an unfamiliar number.

Then he realized it was *Robert Chang's* number.

"Thanks for calling back," Harrison said, feeling as though a lifeline was on the other end. "Your message said you were on vacation."

"I needed to get away, someplace where I could completely forget my troubles at home. But I guess you know all about that."

I do? "What do you mean?" Harrison asked.

There was hesitation, and then Robert said, "I just meant I assume you know about the end of my relationship with your aunt, since you called. Is something wrong? Is she okay?" Harrison heard warmth in the man's voice but also wariness.

It struck then that Harrison wouldn't have known about Robert at all had the dog-walking neighbor not been visiting Lolly when he happened to stop by. Lolly never would have brought up Robert's name. This entire conversation wouldn't be happening.

It was because someone had cared about Lolly and had come to see her. The neighbor with the dog Lolly liked. That meant something, something important in a philosophical sense, but right now Harrison had to focus on the phone call.

"Actually, no," Harrison said. "I'm very sorry to let you know that she's in hospice—at Gentle

Winds here in Prairie City. She was diagnosed with stage-four ovarian cancer about six weeks ago, and it was too late for treatment. Her brother, my father, passed away very recently, and Lolly took a turn for the worse. She's been at Gentle Winds for almost two weeks."

"Oh no," Robert said, his voice unsteady. "I had no idea."

"What happened between you two?" he asked. "I actually don't know. She didn't tell me anything."

"Lolly told me it wasn't working between us after all, and she was sorry but she didn't want to continue seeing me. I was blindsided. She refused to discuss it and wouldn't return my calls or answer the door."

So Harrison was right—Lolly had kept her illness a secret. "When was that—that she ended the relationship?"

"Almost two weeks ago. Must have been the day before she moved to Gentle Winds. Why didn't she tell me? We were getting so close. I thought we were serious."

"I think she didn't want to cause you pain," Harrison said, his chest tightening.

"But she did. I was so broken up I took two weeks' vacation and went to Machu Picchu to immerse myself in another world."

Harrison got it. He'd wanted to do something like that when he'd discovered his ex-girlfriend had been using him. "So things were good between you two until she suddenly ended the relationship?" Harrison asked. That was key.

"Yes. Things were great. I was even thinking of proposing, even though we'd only known each other a few months. Life is short. Unfortunately."

Robert had been thinking of proposing.

Oh, Lolly.

And yes, life was short. Too short. And unfair.

"Robert, I'm going over to see Lolly today. I'll call you back within the hour. I just need to see her first and let her know I've been in touch with you."

"I understand," he said. "I hope you decide to let me see her. I truly love her, Harrison."

His aunt was loved. She hadn't been alone while at Gentle Winds. From a great distance, Robert had loved her, even if Harrison hadn't known it. Somehow, it comforted him.

Harrison pocketed his phone and raced out the door. He couldn't get to Gentle Winds fast enough. But first, he had to text Daisy. He knew she'd want to know what Robert had to say.

He sat in his SUV and sent the text, all but holding his breath while waiting for her to text back. Would she? Maybe she was done with him completely.

He wouldn't blame her.

His phone pinged.

Invite him to visit her!

He wrote back, I'm going to see Lolly now. I'll tell her I think she should let him visit. I just need to see her first.

Sounds good.

He sucked in a breath. She was distancing herself. Of course she was.

I'm sorry for everything, he texted. Not everything. Not all the good stuff.

You can stuff your sorries in a sack, mister, was her reply.

He hung his head, missing her so much his chest ached.

She thought she'd be saving him from a world of hurt, and he was so hurt he had to go on a spiritual quest in Peru! Her plan backfired just like mine did.

Take knife, insert into his chest.

There was so much he wanted to say, to write, but his thumbs were too big to type well on his phone, and nothing he could say—other than the obvious—would get Daisy back in his life.

He knew exactly what she wanted to hear him say: *I would never, could never take the ranch away from you or your family. I thought I could, but I love you and I can't. Even if I didn't love you or respect your siblings, I still couldn't do such a bastardy thing. It's not in me.*

She'd never said that outright, of course, but he knew that was what she wanted. Word for word, really.

If he made things right with Daisy, he'd know deep in his heart for the rest of his life that he'd let down his father. And Lolly.

He leaned his head back against his car's seat rest.

His phone pinged. I have to go—Tony's getting fussy in the bassinet. Good luck.

And that was that.

Harrison gave a gentle knock on Lolly's door at Gentle Winds, but there was no answer, which meant she was napping. He stepped inside, closing the door behind him, then brought the chair he always sat in very close to her bed. He sank down on it.

He looked at her lovely face, her curly blond hair in its little ponytail. Lolly had always looked younger than she was, and the unfairness of it all gripped him hard now. She was only sixty-five. She was too young.

"Aunt Lolly," he said, his voice unsteady. She didn't wake up. He gently shook her shoulder. "Aunt Lolly, it's Harry."

Her eyes fluttered open, and for a moment she looked straight ahead as if she didn't even realize he was there, but then she slightly turned her head, and she strained to smile. "My sweet nephew," she said. She slowly moved her hand to touch his, and he wrapped his around hers. She kept her gaze on him, her eyes so much like his and his dad's.

"Aunt Lolly, remember when your neighbor came to see you? After you fell asleep, she told me you had a boyfriend."

Lolly's face crumpled, and his heart ripped into shreds.

Oh no. No. What had he done? Why had he brought this up? He was the worst. Daisy thought he was the worst? She was right.

"Robert," Lolly whispered. "I hurt him terribly. I told him we were through."

Tears misted her eyes, and she shook her head. *Don't jump in yet*, he told himself. *Let her talk when she's ready.*

"I didn't tell him I was sick," she continued. "Oh, how I miss him, Harry. But it's for the best. He needs to move on."

He almost gasped. It wasn't for the best! Not by a long shot. "Lolly. I took a chance, and I called him. He wants to see you right away."

Her eyes lit up, but she started to cry. "I miss him so much." She wiped at her eyes and then closed them and turned away.

"I'll be right back, Aunt Lolly," he said, not sure if she was even listening.

He went into the hallway. He texted Robert and asked him if he could come to Gentle Winds right now. Robert responded immediately that he would. Harrison was so relieved that he actually felt his shoulder muscles loosen from their knots. He quickly called the reception desk to put Robert Chang on Lolly's visitors' list, then stepped back inside and sat down at Lolly's bedside.

"He's coming, Lolly. Robert is coming to see you."

Her eyes fluttered open again, and she sat up slightly, tilting her head. "He's really coming? Do I look all right?"

He smiled. "You look beautiful. As always."

He could ask about the bet and Bo Dawson, but this wasn't the time. Lolly was emotional and spent enough. He'd wait. Right now, this moment was about the reunion with Robert. Not the past.

He had his fingers crossed that this reunion with

Robert would boost her spirits to the point that Harrison would have more time with her.

Five minutes later, there was a knock on the door. Harrison looked at Lolly, and she nodded, her eyes misty again.

Harrison went to the door and opened it. Robert Chang looked to be around Lolly's age, maybe a bit older. He had thick salt-and-pepper hair and dark eyes and wore round silver eyeglasses. He held a bouquet of red roses. "I'm Harrison McCord. It's very nice to meet you."

Robert extended his hand. "Robert Chang. I can't thank you enough for getting in touch with me." He rushed over to the bed and sat down in the chair Harrison had been sitting in, his gaze misty on Lolly. "I know how you love red roses, Lolly."

"Robert," she whispered, holding out her hand.

He took it in both of his and kissed the back. "I didn't know you were sick. I wish I had. I would have been with you every step of the way. I would have never left your bedside. I love you, Lolly."

"I love you, too, Robert. Too much to burden you with so much sickness and watching me get weaker and weaker. I couldn't do that to you."

Harrison, who'd moved into the bathroom, ostensibly to fill the vase with water for the flowers, but really to give them some privacy, almost broke down.

"But I was wrong, wasn't I?" Lolly said. "I got so used to being alone that I forgot how good it felt to love and be loved, to need and be needed. I thought I could go back to how things were before I met you, but it was terrible. No one should live in the past."

"I'm so grateful your nephew called me." Robert stood up as Harrison came back into the room with the vase of water. He put the flowers in and set them on Lolly's table. "Thank you, again, Harrison."

"Call him Harry," Lolly said with a smile.

Harrison smiled. "Call me Harry," he confirmed to Robert. Then he turned to his aunt. "Love you, Lolly. I'll see you tomorrow morning."

She smiled back, then gave her attention to her beloved.

He left Gentle Winds, everything inside him churning. He'd done right by Lolly. That he knew. He needed to drive with the windows open, feel the wind rushing around him, but he couldn't go back to the ranch right now. He drove aimlessly down Main Street, passing right by Franny's Fish and Chips.

Suddenly he knew where he wanted to be.

He drove to his father's condo. He hadn't sold the apartment yet. Or even emptied it out. Harrison hadn't been able to. He used his key and went inside, taking in the big living room with its sliding glass doors to the back patio, the living room with the black leather couch and his dad's favorite chair, the big black leather electric recliner with its heated seat and massage options. He'd bought the chair for his dad for his birthday four years ago. His father had told him that he often slept in it because it was so great.

He sat down on the recliner and pressed some buttons until the neck and back massage made him say *ahhh*. He reclined back a bit. The chair smelled like his dad, like his aftershave that he always wore. He'd donate a lot of his father's things, but he'd keep this chair and a few other items that represented his dad to him. The navy blue sweater Eric McCord's grandmother had knitted him one Christmas. A painting he fell in love with when they'd been on vacation together in New Orleans. Some family photo albums, though Lolly was the keeper of the ones going back generations.

"Lolly has a boyfriend, Dad," he said into the stillness of the room. "A nice guy named Robert. Came bearing red roses. You would like him." He stared out the window at the big oak. "She wasn't alone, after all. She took a chance on love. And even if it can't be for all that long, she's happy again, Dad."

And Harrison was anything but.

What the hell am I supposed to do? You asked me to get the ranch for you. Your last request. Among your final words, Dad. How do I let that go? How can I? What do I do?

He tried to imagine himself sitting at Franny's Fish and Chips with his father. Telling him this whole story. About Daisy. Her brothers. How Bo Dawson had stayed by eight-year-old Axel's side on a mountain ledge into the wee hours because of a goat. How he'd bequeathed Sara Dawson's mother's garden bed behind the foreman's cabin to her. How he'd never sold Daisy and Noah's mother's wedding rings. Ever. And left them to Daisy in his will, knowing how much they meant to her. He wouldn't leave out the bad parts, either. Selling all their fishing rods, likely for drinking or gambling money. Drunkenly crashing into out-buildings. Loving and leaving women. He'd say it all. The good and the bad.

What would his father say to all that? he wondered. He stared around the room, at the painting from New Orleans. At the big-screen TV where his dad had watched every episode of every iteration of *Law & Order* there was.

He pictured his father sitting across from him, taking a bite of his fried haddock with lettuce and tartar sauce, his side of fries with the spicy mayo. *What would you say, Dad?*

And then it hit him.

He knew exactly what his father would say.

It was like a bolt of lightning struck him.

His father would say, *The ranch belongs to us fair and square. So take ownership—and then sell it back to the Dawsons for a dollar that same day.*

He turned the idea around in his mind. Yes—it would let him honor his father's last wishes *and* let him walk away from the ranch, leaving it with the Dawson family. It was a good compromise. And one he believed his father would approve of.

But taking ownership at all would mean losing Daisy. For her, insisting on taking the ranch would be a betrayal. It was the principle of the thing, and she'd be furious and hurt.

He would lose the love of his life. And he didn't know how he'd ever recover.

Chapter Fourteen

Daisy walked along the creek, Tony in the baby carrier on her chest. It was a gorgeous afternoon, sunny and warm but not humid, the canopy of trees providing lots of shade for her and the baby. She wasn't going to lie—she'd been walking around, particularly in this area of the ranch, because of its proximity to the guest cabins, and because she knew Harrison loved the creek. She'd kept hoping she'd run into him today so that they'd be forced to deal with each other. But she wanted to leave it to chance, because she had no idea what she'd say to him.

She'd been too glad to hear from Sara that he

hadn't checked out today. He'd promised he'd stay through the end of his booking, and he was likely making good on that, even if she'd ordered him out of her house last night. Twice in just a few days, actually.

"What would you do in his place?" Sara had asked earlier. "If Bo had been the best dad in the world and asked you, on his deathbed, to do something for him, something that had always bothered him that he'd left unsettled."

Daisy's mouth had dropped open. "You can't be serious! You think Harrison is right?"

Sara had shaken her head. "No, of course not. But what would you do, Daisy?"

"If everything else was the same? If I'd gotten romantically involved?"

"Yup," Sara had said.

Daisy chewed her lower lip.

"Who would you choose?" Sara pushed. "The man you love or fulfilling your father's last wish?"

"Sara!" Daisy had snapped, more than royally pissed off. But she did stop to think about it. How *could* she choose?

"Sorry, babe, but this is what best friends are for—pointing stuff out even when it's not fun to hear. I'm not trying to play devil's advocate, and

I'm not saying he's right. But neither are you. Just think about it."

She was. And what she was thinking was that Harrison McCord had chosen. And he wasn't choosing her. He wasn't choosing *them*. He knew they had something very special, and he was ready to walk away.

Humph! "So I shouldn't be furious? I shouldn't be scared to death? I shouldn't be brokenhearted or wish I could hate him?"

"Daisy, I'm just asking you to look at it from his perspective. None of us, the Dawson brother I'm married to included, has done that."

Forget her almost relationship with Harrison. Take that out of the equation altogether. Just strictly on the stupid napkin and the *old* condition of the ranch, which was what the napkin had been referring to—the ranch on that date ten years ago—Harrison McCord was dead wrong.

"Because we shouldn't have to!" Daisy protested. "A drunken bet about something that didn't even exist anymore shouldn't be our fault once we rebuilt the ranch. This ranch is not the same one his father won in a bet." The more she thought about that, the more she realized it was true. She'd been truly worried about how any lawyer they'd hire would defend them in court, if need be, and she was pretty sure she'd lit upon it.

The ranch wasn't the same ranch. They weren't the same people. They'd all changed.

Including Bo Dawson. The man who'd left them each personalized letters, bequeathing them something special to them, was not the same man who'd driven them all away, one by one.

"Just putting it out there," Sara had said, squeezing her hand. "Don't be mad at me."

Daisy had hugged her sister-in-law. "I know. And I'm glad you did. Because my mind just went in some new directions."

She'd thought of little else all day. Looking at things through other lenses. Even Harrison's.

Now, Daisy stopped in her tracks along the creek, thunderstruck by something. Somewhere in these days, she'd gone from thinking he couldn't take the ranch from them because it was wrong to thinking he couldn't because it would mean he didn't love her.

Like she loved him.

Harrison McCord wasn't in love with her. He'd lived up to his end of the deal they'd made by sticking around, and she'd "won" because he most certainly did like her and the ranch and the Dawsons that were here. But that was as far as it went for him. He didn't love her.

She closed her eyes and took in a deep breath, dropping her chin down to the top of Tony's head and wishing it reached, because she desperately needed even a chin-to-baby-head hug right now. She turned and headed in the opposite direction, back toward her house. She just wanted to fling herself on her bed and pull the covers over her head for a half hour.

"I'm sorry I've been such a brat," she heard a girl say, and Daisy peered down past the curve on the path, where she could see the mother and teen daughter duo, Christy and Macy Parnell, walking just ahead of her. Sixteen-year-old Macy had blond hair dyed purple on the ends, which looked fabulous. Daisy stopped behind a tree, wanting to give the family privacy and not interrupt them or do anything that would come between their moment. Daisy had caught them bickering several times over the past few days, Macy stomping off in her black Doc Martens. And now here was Macy apologizing for her behavior.

"I'm sorry I haven't been listening, *really* listening," Christy said. "But I really heard you this morning. And I understand how you feel."

Macy hugged her mom. "I'm so glad you talked

me into coming here." Christy put her arm around her daughter, and the two kept walking.

Daisy smiled. At least two people on the ranch were communicating and coming together. She even hoped Tessa and Tom Monello, obnoxious newlyweds, were making compromises they both could smile about.

When Daisy came through the clearing in the trees to turn on the path toward her house, she gasped—because she'd run smack into Harrison McCord. They were so close they'd almost smashed into each other. For once, he was actually dressed for the ranch, in faded jeans, cowboy boots and a navy blue Henley. Maybe that was a bad sign. She hadn't even known he owned cowboy boots. Now he looked like he belonged here. Because he believed the ranch was his?

"I was hoping to run into you," he said. "Not literally. You okay? I didn't bump Tony, did I?"

She shook her head, barely able to form words. Despite being hurt and angry, she still managed to notice how the sunlight glinted in his thick blond hair and on his forearms. How remorseful he looked, the sincere apology in his gorgeous green eyes. How would she ever get over this man?

"The reunion between Lolly and Robert was everything, Daisy. They were both so happy and emotional and just glad to be together again. It's going to change Lolly's last days."

Daisy smiled. "I'm really glad to hear that. A second chance for them both."

"I've come to a decision about the ranch," he said. "One that makes sense to me."

She held her breath and stared at him. "Okay," she said, waiting.

"I'm going to fulfill my father's last request to do right by him and my aunt—then sell the ranch back to you and your brothers for a dollar."

Relief hit her so hard that her knees almost buckled. They wouldn't lose the ranch. Well, they would for a few hours. But they were getting it right back. Unmarred, unchanged.

But then she realized she hadn't been wrong about how Harrison felt—or didn't. He didn't love her. Because if he did, he'd never be able to take ownership—not for a dollar, not for a second. Was she being stubborn? She didn't think so. Sara might. But with everything they'd shared—from Harrison helping to deliver her baby to her helping him find Lolly's mystery boyfriend to those kisses that had made her toes curl—he shouldn't be able to take the ranch, even on paper, even for a few hours. It would always be between them, and she'd always doubt him.

So no, she wasn't being stubborn. She was being realistic.

But they wouldn't lose the ranch.

She cleared her throat. "It's a good compromise." Which it was, really. "I think my brothers will be very relieved. I assume our friendship had something to do with the dollar idea, so thank you for that."

Then, her heart bursting, she walked around him and hurried as fast as she could with a baby strapped to her chest up the path and away from him.

You don't love me.

She had to accept it, and she had no idea how to do that.

Or maybe she did. A new idea started forming. One she wasn't sure about at all. One she wasn't sure that Harrison would agree to. But if she was going to put this all behind her—put Harrison behind her, which she couldn't even imagine—there was only one way she could think of to start.

When Harrison's phone rang ten minutes later, he expected it to be anyone but Daisy. But it was her. He was sitting in the overstuffed chair by the window, staring out at nothing in particular, because all he could see was the look on Daisy's face when she'd barreled past him a little while ago.

She'd still seemed so upset, and he couldn't figure out why. She wasn't getting exactly what she wanted, which would be for him to just tear up that napkin into tiny pieces, but the Dawsons were keeping their ranch. He'd found a way to satisfy both their needs, hadn't he?

"I'd like to visit your aunt," she said. "I want to introduce myself and apologize for my father's behavior."

He stood up, clutching his phone a little too tightly. "I don't know, Daisy. Now Lolly is reunited with Robert. I'm not sure I should even bring up bad old memories. I'm comfortable with how I'll proceed with the napkin and the ranch. I don't think I need to even mention it to Lolly. It has no bearing, no place in her life right now."

But he realized with absolute clarity that he *did* want to introduce Daisy to Lolly. His aunt was his last surviving relative, and Daisy meant so much to him. He wanted them to know each other, however briefly. However briefly he had Daisy in his life, too.

"Oh," she said. "Okay." She sounded so disappointed.

"Actually, I would love for you to meet her.

But as someone close to me. Not as Bo Dawson's daughter. I mean, I know that's who you are. And I'm sure your name will register with Lolly. But, Daisy, you're also—"

"Also what?"

The woman who means so much to me that I can't think straight. "Forget what I just said. You're everything you are, including Bo's daughter and all that that means. Are you free to go see Lolly now?" he asked, hoping she wouldn't press him on the *also*.

She hesitated, and because he did know her so well, he was one hundred percent sure that she was deciding whether or not to demand he finish what he'd been about to say.

"I'm free now. Axel can watch Tony. He actually just asked a few minutes ago if he could take Tony on a walk, and I know he has a few free hours. I think he's hoping to run into Hailey when she returns from leading the wilderness tour. To apologize in person."

He recalled the way Hailey practically flew out the door last night when things got really out of hand. "So Axel didn't go with the group? I guess with the way things went last night, it probably wouldn't happen."

"Hailey told Axel that our ranch hand Dylan

had already asked another hand to join and that they were all set for an extra expert," Daisy explained. "I think Hailey is probably going to cross Axel off her crush list. At least for right now. And I think I'll hang up my matchmaking hat."

"Sorry," he said. "I know you were hoping a romance would give him a reason to stay in town." Besides, Axel didn't strike Harrison as all that interested in a relationship anyway. He knew another lone wolf when he saw one, and Axel Dawson was very much on his own right now—and wanted to be.

"Here we are," she said, "chatting away like everything's just peachy between us. How does that keep happening?"

"Because at the core, we're true friends, Daisy. And no matter what else, there is something very special between us."

"Fat lot of good that's gonna do us," she said.

She had a point, but he didn't want to think about that or talk about it. "I'll pick you up in fifteen minutes."

"See you then."

When she ended the call, he kept the phone in his hand for a moment to keep even a semblance of connection to her.

He really hoped introducing her to his aunt

wouldn't go terribly wrong. That Lolly wouldn't hear the name Dawson, recall the name Daisy as one of her ex-boyfriend's kids and become agitated.

For a man who'd always been sure of himself, he was doing an awful lot of questioning and second-guessing.

As Daisy walked beside Harrison into the Gentle Winds hospice, she realized her hands were shaking. What if Lolly didn't accept her apology? What if she told Daisy to get out?

"Harrison, maybe this isn't a good idea. If I upset Lolly, I'll never be able to forgive myself."

"Emotionally, she's in a good place. I think this might even give her a sense of closure. Not just about her past, but because of how my father held on to it—the bitterness, all of it. It'll allow her to put that part of her life away for good, you know?"

"That makes sense," she said. "Thanks." She looked down at her hands, which were a lot less trembly. Phew.

From the moment he'd picked her up at the house until now, there hadn't been any time or space to focus on them, which was a good thing.

They stopped at the elevator. "Robert is visiting Lolly right now. I texted him, and he'll step out when we get there. He added that he hates leaving her side for a minute."

"That's some love story," Daisy said. "I'm so glad that worked out the way it did."

If only ours could.

They arrived at Lolly's room, and Harrison gave a soft knock. Robert came out and shook Harrison's hand. After introductions, Robert said he'd go to the cafeteria for a while and for Harrison to let him know when they were heading out. Robert struck Daisy as kind, polite and warm, and meeting him helped buoy her right now.

When Harrison pushed open the door, Daisy's heart started hammering. *Please let this go well*, she thought.

Lolly was sitting up, lots of pillows behind her, and there was a bouquet of red roses on the table. Daisy definitely saw the family resemblance in the two McCords—particularly the gorgeous green eyes. Lolly's hair was ash blond and just past her chin.

"Aunt Lolly, I'd like to introduce you to someone special. This is Daisy Dawson. Daisy, my aunt Lolly."

Lolly peered at Daisy, then at Harrison. "Special?" she asked with a sly smile.

"Yes, special," Harrison said. "We'll leave it at that."

Lolly raised an eyebrow, a gleam in her eyes. "I know how that goes." She smiled and then held out her hand toward Daisy.

A whoosh of relief flooded through Daisy. Lolly was funny and kind. Maybe the woman hadn't heard her last name clearly or connected it to the man who'd broken her heart ten years ago, but for now, Daisy felt a lot more comfortable. She took Lolly's hand, and Lolly gave it a light squeeze.

"Come sit," Lolly said.

Daisy sat down beside the bed. Harrison was standing behind her, and she could feel his hands on the back of her chair. Bracing himself, she knew.

"Dawson, huh?" Lolly said. "Any relation to Bo Dawson of Bear Ridge?"

Daisy bit her lip and sucked in a breath. "My father."

"Really?" Lolly exclaimed, looking from Daisy to Harrison. "Did you know I used to date your dad? About ten years ago."

Oh boy, did she know. "Yes. Harrison told me."

"Is he still as good-looking as ever?" Lolly asked. "Don't tell Robert I said that." She winked at Daisy.

Daisy almost gasped. *She's not upset. She's not demanding I leave at once.*

"Well, he actually passed away back in December," Daisy said.

Lolly patted Daisy's hand. "I'm sorry to hear that. The two of us didn't have a happy ending, but that's how things go. Sometimes they work, sometimes they don't. Took me a long time to let go of him, but that's also how things go."

"I'm sorry he hurt you so badly," Daisy said, hoping she wasn't overstepping by saying so.

"Well, in the end, the very end, I learned what was important and nonnegotiable to me in a relationship. Someone I could count on. Trust. Took me a while to trust myself, but when I finally let go of the past, I found everything I wanted in Robert. I almost lost him because I was so stubborn, but Harry here saved the day. Sometimes you have to know better than the people who *think* they know better. Right, Harry?"

Harrison moved beside Daisy and bent down to give his aunt a kiss. "You're absolutely right."

Daisy wondered if Lolly knew about the bet. In fact, she just realized that Harrison's aunt might not know anything about it. Her protective brother might have tried to avenge his sister's broken heart, the strain on her bank account and the loss of her friendship with the woman Bo had been three-timing with, on the down low.

"Ah, there I go getting all tired again," Lolly said. "I keep falling asleep on poor Robert as he talks or reads to me, but does that man have a melodic voice or what?" She smiled, her green eyes that reminded Daisy so much of Harrison's twinkling.

"We'll let you rest," Harrison said.

Daisy stood. She gently squeezed Lolly's hand. "I'm so glad I met you."

"Me, too," Lolly said. "And I'm very happy that Harry has someone so special in his life."

Daisy felt tears sting her eyes. She managed something of a smile, and then Harrison was ushering her out.

In the hallway the dam burst, and tears streamed down her face, and Harrison held her. She swiped at her eyes and got herself together. "I'm okay. Text Robert to come back. I don't want them to miss too much time together."

Harrison smiled and nodded. He texted Robert, and then they headed out.

The sunshine and fresh air felt good on her face. "I can't believe I just cried like that. I guess I'm crying over a lot of different things for a lot of different reasons."

"You can always be yourself with me, Daisy," he said as they walked to his SUV. "Happy, sad—the gamut. Angry, too. And I know I've made you angry."

"I don't want to talk about that anymore. It's settled, right? We keep the ranch, so all's good with that."

They both got inside and buckled up. "And what about us? I know we're not friends," he said with a smile. "But we're something, right?"

He was doing what he felt was right. For his family and for himself. He'd take the ranch, then sell it right back to them. But she couldn't live with that. The man who loved her would rip up the napkin. Call her stubborn. She'd been about to settle for a life with a husband who didn't love her so that Tony would grow up with his father. She wasn't about to settle again.

She didn't respond and he didn't press her, just drove out of the Gentle Winds parking lot. She figured he was digesting all that Lolly had said. His aunt had said quite a lot.

And Daisy was trying not to think about the moment Harrison would check out of Cabin No. 1 and she'd never see him again.

Chapter Fifteen

As Harrison pulled up to Daisy's house, Axel came out with Tony in his arms. The little guy was wearing a blue-and-white onesie, a tiny straw cowboy hat on his head. Man, that was cute.

"He's officially a cowboy now," Axel said as Daisy stepped out of the car.

Harrison wondered if he should just drive off or get out and talk to Axel. The last time hadn't gone well. But things were at least settled now as far as the ranch was concerned. Axel wouldn't be asking Harrison to punch him in the face.

He got out of the car and came around. "Hey, Tony. I like your hat."

Axel gave Harrison something of a smile, which was a big improvement over the usual scowl and death stare. "It's lined in very soft cotton to keep his little head safe."

"I love it," Daisy said. "Thanks, Uncle Axel. And thanks for watching him."

Axel nodded at his sister, then turned to Harrison. "So I hear you're going to sell us back the ranch for a dollar thirty seconds after you take ownership." He extended his hand, and Harrison shook it. "It's a good compromise, and on behalf of my brothers, we appreciate it. You certainly didn't have to do that. But we're damned glad you are."

"It's the right thing to do. I'm satisfied, and I think my father would be, too."

Axel handed over Tony to Daisy. "I'm headed out with Noah to look at a new hay baler. See you later, little nephew." He nodded at Daisy and Harrison and got in his truck.

"Your brothers believe it's a good compromise, Daisy. I wish you could see it that way. It's the best thing I can do in the situation."

Her eyes flashed. "You've made your decision. We're through talking about the ranch, then. You're checking out today, right?"

"Right," he said, his heart shredding as he stood there.

"Then I guess this is goodbye. Wave goodbye to Harrison, Tony," she said to the baby.

Okay, now his heart just completely tore into pieces.

She turned and walked up the porch steps, Tony's little cowboy hat bopping a bit.

He wanted to follow her inside and talk, but what was there to say? He got back in the SUV and drove down to the cabin. He didn't want to leave this place. This ranch. He didn't want to say goodbye to Daisy or Tony.

He stood in the main room of his cabin, taking in the walls, the furnishings, the care that had gone into building this cabin—rebuilding it. He thought about the main house and the barns and the animals. He could barely believe he'd shown up here planning to wrest the ranch away from the Dawsons—and not sell it back—but he himself had been a different person then. A person holding on to bitterness—from his breakup with the woman who'd used him to his grief over losing his dad and then being faced with losing his aunt.

Now he was losing Daisy. And nothing about that was right. He felt like Lolly must have ten years ago, giving up on love and romance because she'd been so hurt and betrayed. Then giving up on love a second time, breaking her own heart because she didn't want the man she loved to have to deal with all the pain, angst and suffering.

Sometimes you have to know better than the people who think *they know better. Right, Harry?*

That applied to a few different scenarios, he thought, his head about to explode.

It's wrong to take the ranch at all, Dad, he realized with such force of clarity that he had to sit down as the truth sank in. *It's wrong to take the ranch because it's not ours—never was. For a lot of reasons.*

But one of the biggest reasons was that the Dawsons had invested in rebuilding and had made it happen—the ranch wasn't the same one Bo had bet and lost. That ranch was gone. And all those old, bad memories weren't used in the renovations.

Harrison knew better now, and that was all that mattered. That had nothing to do with honoring or dishonoring his father; it had to do with what was truly right. Whether Lolly had been speaking of the bet and the ranch when she'd said that people had to know better than the people who thought they knew better, he had no idea. He wasn't sure if she even knew about the bet. He didn't think so, but she did seem to be trying to tell him something important.

Another reason, perhaps the one that mattered

most: he'd fallen in love with Daisy Dawson and couldn't touch her family's history and legacy and present and future. The ranch belonged to the Dawsons—fair and square.

He was pretty sure he'd already lost her, for not having understood this before now, when it was likely too late. But he couldn't wait to tell her.

That was some cruddy goodbye, Daisy thought as she helped herself to one of Cowboy Joe's chocolate-chunk scones. Heartbreak eating, for sure. At this rate, she'd never lose the baby weight, but she'd rather have the scone than fit into her old jeans right now.

Harrison's handsome face, and tousled blond hair and warm green eyes flashed in her mind, and she took a big bite of the scone. Could she really let that awful goodbye be it? The last time she'd see him? Talk to him? *We did have something, something very special, and I may be upset, but that was goodbye. We went through too much together for that.*

They did. Oh foo, she was going after him. At least to say a kinder goodbye, one that she could feel good about when she thought about Harrison in the days and weeks and months to come. Oh God, maybe years.

She sipped her water. "Looks like we're going for a walk down to Harrison's cabin," she said to Tony, who was being adorable by just existing in his bassinet.

She strapped the Snugli on to her chest and then scooped up her boy and put him inside.

She wanted to put on the precious and tiny cowboy hat Axel had bought his nephew, but the brim was a touch too wide to fit while he was in the carrier, so she put a floppy white sun hat on Tony's head. "Let's go see Harrison and say a goodbye we both deserve. That man helped bring you into the world. He made my stir-fry and secret recipe rice when my lower back was aching. He made me believe I could love again—he *made* me love again. And like his wise aunt Lolly said, sometimes it doesn't work out."

She walked down the path, holding back tears, hoping he hadn't already packed and left. She needed one last Harrison McCord hug. A real goodbye. And then she'd focus on Tony and her family and the ranch and maybe ease back into her duties as guest relations manager early so that Sara could take on the job as forewoman sooner than she'd expected. Her sister-in-law was so excited about the promotion. Between the great sitter they all used and one another, there'd be solid childcare for Tony and his little cousins.

"Daisy!"

She turned around and saw the newlyweds, Tessa and Tom Monello, waving and hurrying over to her. They were in their city clothes, sharp and monochromatic, Tessa's heels at least three inches. How she didn't sink into the grass was beyond Daisy.

"We're checking out today," Tessa said, "but we both wanted to thank you for that dinner party from hell, which actually ended up saving our marriage! We talked for hours that night. And we're going to see a marriage counselor at home and make sure we work through our differences. You were right when you said that what mattered was our love for each other, and we've got that by the truckload."

"I'm really happy to hear that," Daisy said. Dinner party from hell? Yeah, she'd agree with that.

"Tessa, I still can't believe you could have one of these adorable tykes and you want to wait," Tom said to his wife as he made peekaboo faces at Tony. "But I'm willing to wait until you're ready. As long as it's not *that* long."

Tessa bopped him on the arm, slipping her hand in his. "Thanks, Daisy. We had a great time here. The ranch is really beautiful and restful."

She watched the Monellos kiss their way up the path toward their cabin, so wistful she just stood there staring long after they disappeared down the slope.

"It's amazing they didn't trip," said a familiar male voice.

Harrison! "I was just coming to see you. To say a proper goodbye. Yes, I'm mad at you, but whatever."

"I was just coming to see you."

"For the same reason?" she asked. At least he wasn't going to just leave with things so awful between them. Yeah, they weren't friends—although, dammit, they were—but they needed to smooth things over for peace of mind. For both of them.

"Actually," he said, "I'm hoping you won't say goodbye, Daisy. Because the thought of losing you—for real and for good—made me realize I can't. I can't lose you."

Her heart pinged with hope. This was a very good start.

"I love my dad, but I love you, too," he continued. "And I love that little boy right here. I can't bear the thought of taking the ranch, even on paper for an hour. I respect you and your brothers too much for that. Like you said, the ranch isn't the one your father bet. And none of us is the same person." He stepped closer and took both of her hands in his. He kissed each one. "I love you, Daisy Dawson. So, so much. And I love Tony Lincoln Dawson. With all my heart."

Daisy gasped. "Did you hear that, Tony? He loves us!"

Harrison reached into his jacket pocket and pulled out the napkin. Her father's handwriting made her smile instead of want to cry. Then he ripped the napkin into pieces and shoved the mess into his pants pocket. "I wanted to throw up the pieces like confetti but then realized one of the employees would have to clean it up. I also thought about just giving you the napkin as some kind of weird keepsake, but this is part of a bitter past, and I think it's better just gone."

Someone pinch me. Can this really be happening? "I agree, Harrison." She put her arms around him, the baby between them. "I love you so much."

He tilted his head down and kissed her, then looked into her eyes, and she saw so much in his— love, desire, happiness, relief, warmth…her future. "My dad would be standing up on his recliner chair and cheering me right now. I know it's true. Why didn't I realize that before? I have no doubt Lolly would be, too."

Daisy reached up on her tiptoes and kissed him.

"I'm doing that now, too—in my head. So is Tony. And my brothers. And Sara. I'll bet even Cowboy Joe is cheering you."

He laughed. "I want us to be a family. You, me and Tony—oh and your five brothers and their wives, when they get them. I never want to leave this ranch, because I love it. Not because it was ever mine or my family's. I love the Dawson Family Guest Ranch, and I love you."

"Let's go home, then," Daisy said and they turned toward the farmhouse, hand in hand.

* * * * *

*Don't miss the next Dawson Family Ranch book,
available July 2020 from
Harlequin Special Edition!*

*And don't miss these other great books
featuring single parents:*

Her Motherhood Wish
by Tara Taylor Quinn

Date of A Lifetime
by Lynne Marshall

Fortune's Greatest Risk
by Marie Ferrarella

*Available now wherever Harlequin
Special Edition books and ebooks are sold!*

"Gracie, will you look at me?"

Stifling a sigh, she turned her head to face him. Those
melty brown eyes were full of self-recrimination and
regret.

"I'm sorry," he said. "I never should have touched you.
I'm too old for you, and I'm not any kind of relationship
material, anyway. I don't know what got into me, but I
swear to you it's never going to happen again."

Hmm. How to respond?

Too bad there wasn't a large blunt object nearby. The
guy deserved a hard bop on the head. What was wrong
with him? No wonder it hadn't worked out with Marjorie.
The man didn't have a clue.

But never mind. Gracie held it together as he
apologized some more. She watched that beautiful mouth

move and pondered the mystery of how such a great guy could have his head so far up his own ass.

Maybe if she yanked him close and kissed him, he'd get over himself and admit that last night had been amazing, the two of them had off-the-charts chemistry and he didn't want to walk away from all that goodness, after all.

Yeah, kissing him might shut him up and get him back on track for more hot sexy times. It had worked more than once already.

But come on. She couldn't go jumping on him and smashing her mouth on his every time he started beating himself up for having a good time with her.

No. A girl had to have a little pride.

He thought last night was a mistake?

Fair enough. She'd actually let herself believe for a minute or two there that they had something good going on, that her long dry spell manwise might be over.

But never mind about that. Let him have it his way. She would agree with him.

And then she would show him exactly what he was missing. And then, when he couldn't take it anymore and begged her for another chance, she would say that they couldn't, that he was too old for her and it wouldn't be right.

Don't miss
Their Secret Summer Family *by Christine Rimmer,*
available May 2020 wherever
Harlequin Special Edition books and ebooks are sold.

Harlequin.com